D1263993

SPECIAL MESSAGE TO READERS

THE ULVERSCROFT FOUNDATION
(registered UK charity number 264873)

was established in 1972 to provide funds for research, diagnosis and treatment of eye diseases. Examples of major projects funded by the Ulverscroft Foundation are:-

- The Children's Eye Unit at Moorfields Eye Hospital, London
- The Ulverscroft Children's Eye Unit at Great Ormond Street Hospital for Sick Children
- Funding research into eye diseases and treatment at the Department of Ophthalmology, University of Leicester
- The Ulverscroft Vision Research Group, Institute of Child Health
- Twin operating theatres at the Western Ophthalmic Hospital, London
- The Chair of Ophthalmology at the Royal Australian College of Ophthalmologists

You can help further the work of the Foundation by making a donation or leaving a legacy. Every contribution is gratefully received. If you would like to help support the Foundation or require further information, please contact:

THE ULVERSCROFT FOUNDATION
The Green, Bradgate Road, Anstey
Leicester LE7 7FU, England
Tel: (0116) 236 4325

website: www.foundation.ulverscroft.com

DAISY'S DILEMMA

London, 1822: Lady Daisy's machinations to get Mr John Brent to propose marriage to her have finally come to fruition — but she's surprised to find herself underwhelmed and even a little disappointed. Her distant cousin and resident musician, Reuben Longreach, recognises Daisy's fiercely intelligent and independent nature — which would be wasted on marriage to a dullard — and hatches plans of his own to thwart her engagement before she makes what he calls a 'wrong choice'. Will Daisy learn to listen to her heart before it's too late?

Books by Anne Stenhouse
in the Linford Romance Library:

MARIAH'S MARRIAGE

ANNE STENHOUSE

DAISY'S DILEMMA

Complete and Unabridged

LINFORD
Leicester

First published in Great Britain in 2015

First Linford Edition
published 2017

A catalogue record for this book is available from the British Library.

ISBN 978–1–4448–3259–4

Published by
F. A. Thorpe (Publishing)
Anstey, Leicestershire

Set by Words & Graphics Ltd.
Anstey, Leicestershire
Printed and bound in Great Britain by
T. J. International Ltd., Padstow, Cornwall

This book is printed on acid-free paper

1

London, 1822

'He comes as a conquering hero.'

'What?' Daisy Longreach lifted her chocolate-coloured gaze from contemplation of a hothouse peach to her companion's more sanguine stare. 'Who comes?'

Reuben sighed, and Daisy wondered if he'd preceded the remark about conquering heroes with something a little less impenetrable which, because she was enjoying her breakfast for the first time in nearly a week, she'd missed.

'The town seems to be full of conquering heroes, and —' She thought of her future sister-in-law. '— their ladies. You will have to be more specific.'

Daisy decided her disordered digestion was restored enough to attempt the peach, and reached for a clean fruit knife. Reuben reached, too, and his beautiful musician's fingers closed round her wrist, trapping her hand and forcing her attention fully onto his face.

She'd known Reuben all her life, and yet in that moment she wondered if she'd ever *truly* known him. The heat from his hand travelled along her arm and she was nonplussed. No one ever laid hands on her without a specific purpose, like Smithers dressing her hair or Stephens handing her into the town coach. Reuben held her gaze and her hand.

'Reuben?' she queried in a small voice. Then, because she saw no reason to bow before her elder's ill humour, she spoke more sharply. 'I warn you, I have not enjoyed my food for nearly a week, and it puts you in grave danger to get between me and my breakfast.'

'Your breakfast has been substantial. It might not be sensible to add fruit, which is high in acid content.' He spoke with calm deliberation.

'Your seriousness makes me uneasy, sir. Have peaches been discovered to cause widespread illness and distress?'

'Not to the same extent as oysters,' Reuben replied. 'Ah, I see you are still conscious of the effect of making a wrong choice. Your complexion blanches.'

Daisy drew her hand from his grasp and sat back in her chair. They were alone in the breakfast parlour of the family's house in Grosvenor Square. She assumed her brother, Toby, had eaten earlier, and Mama always kept to her room until nearly midday. Reuben clearly wanted to make her understand something, and it had nothing to do with peaches or oysters.

'Wrong choices? You think I should cancel my trip to Spain with Mama?'

'Your trip to Spain has been designed solely to bring Mr John Brent to heel, and now that he comes to ask for your hand, it will not be necessary.' Reuben ground the words out as if he was addressing a particularly backward infant. 'You've kept him dangling these several months, but he will make his move today, Daisy. Be sure you give him the right answer, won't you?'

'John comes to ask for my hand? What can you mean, Reuben? Neither Toby nor Mama has asked me whether I wish to receive John Brent.' She pushed back vigorously and her chair crashed to the floor. How dare Reuben make sport with her feelings like this? He must guess how strong they were in relation to John — and unhappily, that John's proud nature would not allow him to accept he might live on her inheritance.

'Your brother will be back shortly. He is receiving Brent now. That is why I take this opportunity to remind you of the consequences of wrong choices, Daisy.' Reuben was on his feet too now, and she had to look up. There was no doubt of his seriousness in addressing her.

'Reuben, we have been friends since childhood, but this is not a matter for you. My choice of a husband —'

'Will, at present, be influenced by the derring-do Brent has found himself involved with. It has left him looking more heroic than he normally does,' Reuben snapped. 'Do not think he sought his injuries.'

'Injuries? John has been injured? I

knew he was with Toby and the others when they ...' She hesitated. The men had gone off after Toby's betrothed, Mariah Fox, and in an ensuing fight, Sir Lucas Wellwood had been killed. Toby was much engaged in talks with the law officers, trying to convince them of the accidental nature of the knife thrust that took Wellwood's life. Because Toby had also been the unwitting user of an untipped blade that led to the death of his older brother, causing him to succeed as earl, the whole affair was proving protracted. No one had told Daisy that John had been injured.

'It is too much to be borne,' she said angrily. 'Not only am I kept in ignorance of the true nature of last week's events, but I am expected to decide on my future with as much warning as if I were choosing a new gown.' She moved away from Reuben, and when she had gathered her thoughts to ask about the nature of John's injuries, turned back to face him. Behind Reuben, the door opened and Toby strode through the space.

'Ah, Daisy. I have some news which I hope will clear the thunder massing in your eyes,' her brother said, and Daisy knew then Reuben was right — John Brent would come to ask for her hand. It was the most prized of all her desires — so why did she swing her gaze from Toby's to Reuben's in search of answers?

'Perhaps you would leave us for a moment, Reuben,' she said.

She saw the frown crease Toby's face while Reuben made a small, tight bow and left the room. Her brother's eyes held enquiry, but she kept her counsel. She had longed for this moment since the first evening party she'd attended after leaving the schoolroom two years ago. John Brent wanted to marry her. She smiled at her brother. She was ready.

* * *

'You are asking me to marry you?' Daisy addressed the man kneeling in front of her. She continued to be surprised. She was a tiny bit relieved. She was, unexpectedly, disappointed. Emotions tumbled around in her head, as unwelcome as the disordered digestion that had laid her low for nearly five days. She didn't find herself in the best fettle for dealing with marriage proposals.

John Brent raised his head from kissing her fingers and smiled. Daisy sighed. There was no doubt but John's smile threatened to churn her recovering insides all over again. The cool turquoise of his eyes displaced the memory of Reuben's dark ones snapping with angry amber chips. What right had Reuben to be angry with her? she wondered.

'Yes, my beloved Daisy. I am asking for your hand.' John stood, bringing her whole attention back to him. Her gaze followed his rise. His was such a comfortably rounded figure that she sometimes forgot how very tall he was. 'Isn't this what we have both wished for?'

She dragged her attention back from contemplating the joys of a suitor who was not dwarfed by her Mellon heritage, to the problem at hand. John was finally proposing to her — as Reuben, irritated and angry, had told her he would.

'Certainly, it is a matter we have discussed.' She stood up too and, evading the hand John stretched toward her waist, crossed from the morning room fireplace to one of the great windows overlooking the gardens behind the house. It was unnerving to have Reuben's admonition about the consequences of wrong choices in her head, souring the moment that for many months had been the focus of her existence. Perhaps that uncomfortable conversation prompted her reply to John now.

'You were not disposed to make an offer as recently as Mama's evening party last Sunday week.'

She did not turn back to John as she spoke, so could only guess at his reaction from the sharp intake of breath. Perhaps her sally was a little unkind, but his intransigence over the matter of living on her inheritance had taken its toll on both their sensibilities.

'Am I to understand your position over

my allowance has shifted?' she asked. The words sounded peevish. While she had been frustrated by John's honourable behaviour in refusing to live on her money, she'd relished the prospect of wearing him down and securing his suit. It chimed very well with the details of a three-volume romance she was engaged in creating. Now he seemed to have come round without any sacrifice being required of her. She would no longer have to go to Spain with her mama. The visit to an elderly Spanish relative they had identified as a possible suitor, with the sole intention of inflaming John's jealousy, would not be necessary. It was vexing at best and impossible at worst. Would Mama still expect her to make the journey? Lady Mellon professed a great keenness to see her native land.

'No, you should not understand that,' John said sharply, interrupting Daisy's meandering thoughts. 'I am still of the belief that I must support my wife out of my own resources. M'sisters, too.' He came to stand close behind her, and she was conscious of warmth enveloping her. The day was hot and John was wearing tight-fitting formal clothing. He accorded her every decent attention a girl should expect when a proper offer of matrimony was being discussed.

His clothes were impeccable. The flowers he'd sent earlier in the day now filled several vases, and their scents perfumed the air delightfully. He had spoken to her elder brother, Toby, and sent a note to her mama. Something in John's circumstances had altered. As was entirely usual, no one had thought to inform her of it.

'The ructions around Toby and Mariah have pushed my news into the background,' John said, and he took a deep breath. 'Coal has been found on some land m'father bought in the north, near Newcastle. The seams are rich and already profitable.'

Daisy turned to him, caught up in his excitement, but her gaze lighted on his face and she started, having forgotten his injuries. There was a huge scar on his temple, and bruising covered his forehead and most of the left side of his face. The surgeon had cut a lot of hair away in order to clean the wound, and John looked piratical. Even today, five days after the fight with Lucas Wellwood, he was paler than his normal florid colouring. He swayed a little, and Daisy instinctively grasped his elbow to steady him.

'We are neither of us in the pink,' she joked, although she'd had to stifle her shock when she'd first seen him earlier that morning. 'Let us sit down again.'

She led the way back to the sofas at the fireplace and sat, drawing John gently down to her side. His breathing was a little irregular, and there was the sheen of sweat on his forehead. The ructions had been violent indeed.

'Toby did not tell me you were injured before this morning,' she said carefully. The earl was keeping much of the event to himself. He had only said Lucas had been killed in a fight.

'We did not want to cause you any more discomfort when you were already ill,' John replied, and she watched his gaze slide away to study the portrait of a long-dead Mellon ancestor in whom he could have no possible interest. Did he also think he would shield her from the whole story?

'The first earl — something of a bore, if one believes all the diaries written by his wife and daughters,' Daisy said of the man in the portrait, hoping to bring John's attention back to her.

'Lucas Wellwood turned out to be much more of a blackguard than we had reason to expect. Devious, we knew, but also organised and cruel. He thrust his foot out and I tumbled over it at full pelt. I hit the edge of a desk. He threatened Mariah.' John rushed the words out and stopped. He brought his eyes, now ringed with tears, back to Daisy, and she waited. 'He had already threatened you.'

'Me!' she exclaimed in horror. There had been an air of menace whenever Wellwood was in the company, but Toby had promised to keep him away. Her brother had sworn that the man would never be one of their family.

'Toby will berate me, but I think you should know the bones of the villain's plans at the very least.' John raised an arm and placed it around Daisy's shoulders.

She felt him wince. 'You have other injuries?'

'They are minor and will heal.' He squeezed her shoulder and she smiled in response. 'Wellwood intended to abduct you, my dear Daisy. He was wallowing in debt, and when his plan to marry his sister to Toby and steal the Mellon tiara melted away, he became deranged with fury.'

'I cannot understand this. I would never have agreed to marry Lucas Wellwood. How could he expect to achieve such a thing?'

'You have had a lot of freedom in the use of the carriage and suchlike. Walking out with only Smithers for company,' John said tentatively.

'My maid is formidable. She grew up in the Foundling Hospital, you know.'

'I do know; you have mentioned the

matter more than once, m'dear. The point is, when faced with the kind of roughs Wellwood had hired, she and you would have been easily overcome.'

'I would never have consented to be Wellwood's wife. Never.'

'Your eyes flash fire and you are as strong as any young woman might be, but none of that would have saved you from ...' John tailed off, and Daisy began to understand. He was hinting that Wellwood had contemplated dishonouring her.

'Wellwood was a gentleman. He would never force his attentions on an unwilling lady.' Even as she spoke the words, she knew they were naive and misguided. She remembered some bruising on his sister's arm. The air became chill.

'Wellwood was a gentleman by birth. By nature, he was as far from that status as the beasts in fields. He had killed at least one woman before; a parlour maid, I believe.' John drew back his arm and sat up straighter. There was nothing of his usual bluff manner evident when he spoke of the late baronet.

'He is dead now, and you and the others will recover,' she said.

John shrugged. The action alarmed her. 'Was there more damage? Mariah has been to see me, and she appears to beas well as one might be after such an event.'

'Do not fret, Daisy. The future countess was very little harmed. However, one of our men has a broken nose, and another lost a lot of blood. Mariah applied a tourniquet and undoubtedly saved his life.'

'Goodness. Mariah had an exciting time,' Daisy said, and instantly regretted the words. Her brother's betrothed had been in danger of her life, and her maid, Tilly, too. 'I am sorry. That sounded flippant, and I do not mean to be, but I have languished in my room for nearly a week.'

She saw John's brow crease and took a deep breath. Her thoughts were discomposed, and she was struggling to find the right words to console him. Normally, they crossed swords over their differences about her inheritance, but today that contention had been removed and she was at a loss.

'Perhaps we have kept too much information from you, dearest Daisy, but it was with the best of motives,' John said stiffly.

'Did you intend to hide away for the time it takes to heal those scars?'

'That was Toby's wish, but I had sought his permission to address you before the fracas, and I could not wait a moment longer.' He pulled out his pocket handkerchief and wiped his face. 'How would you have felt if you had read of the changing Brent fortunes in the *Times* but had not received an offer from me?'

The remark struck home. Daisy would have been most upset to read of such a thing and yet not to have received an offer. She looked into John's eyes and was surprised by an expression there she had not seen before. His gaze was fixed on her and his eyes flashed with light. She sat back against the cushions, but he did not drop his gaze from her face.

Daisy flushed with an unaccustomed heat. John desired her.

'It was brave of you to travel from

Richmond while in such pain, John. I am conscious of the great honour you do me in offering me your hand, and I . . .' Daisy hesitated. This was the biggest decision any woman of her class ever made. Toby would not force her to accept John if she did not wish to marry him. Even her mama would concur, although she would be sorely out of patience. Daisy looked up at the big man waiting in nervous anticipation for her reply.

'Be sure you give him the right answer, won't you?' Reuben's clipped words of earlier teased her memory.

How dare he?

She reminded herself that John was undoubtedly the love of her life — but her life had so far been short. That was the dilemma she was faced with in accepting the first proposal made to her. It was final and could not be altered.

Blood trickled down the side of John's face, and he swatted it impatiently with the handkerchief. Daisy thought how very like him that unconscious action was. His gaze never left hers, and searched her soul. How could she fail to react to this evidence of his bravery in her defence?

'I am minded to accept, sir. I would be foolish indeed to allow such a conquering hero to escape,' she said as she took the cloth from him and dabbed the blood. 'It could be some time before another rides this way.'

* * *

Daisy was overwhelmed by the reaction to their betrothal. John whooped with delight, causing yet more blood to seep from his injury, and the door of the morning room was flung wide. Her mama, Toby, and one or two of the sundry relatives who always seemed to be living with them fell through. She could see Stephens and Mrs Burtles hovering in the background. Reuben, too. He peeled his long frame off the opposite wall.

'Well done, Brent, well done, indeed,' Toby roared as if the world had become deaf and John had conquered something. Daisy gazed in bemusement around her.

'Darling,' her mama said, 'I am so very happy for you.'

'Thank you, Mama. How could I refuse when John has done so much to uphold my honour?' She cast her betrothed a shy glance under her lashes and saw his quick blush of embarrassment.

'Really, Daisy, it was a joint effort,' said John. 'We all worked it out together, didn't we, Toby?'

'We did,' Toby replied, but the glance he cast toward John was guarded, as if he was testing how much of their story he'd revealed to Daisy. She bristled. Why did all her relatives regard her as a feather-brained child?

But then she realised that as well as her recent adventures, Mariah was able to tell everyone how much she loved teaching. Daisy was acutely aware that she herself had nothing to call her own. Shopping and dancing suddenly seemed frivolous beyond anything. If she married John before the summer was over and fell with child immediately, she would never step out of her pampered existence. They would all go on assuming she had no strength of character.

'Will you have a double wedding?' a voice asked from the fringes of the family group.

'No!' Daisy exclaimed with more heat than was seemly. 'You are too provoking, Reuben. What lady wishes to share her most special day with another?'

'One who is anxious to tie the knot,' John said, and the warmth in his voice caused Toby to blink and Lady Mellon to cough. Daisy glanced at his overheated face and wondered whether the blows to his head had affected his sensibilities.

'John,' she said in a low voice, 'Mariah and Toby have their plans much advanced, and we would do them a disservice to force ourselves into them.'

'If you say so, my love, but I would be happy to take such a path.'

'I think not, Mr Brent,' Lady Mellon said forcefully. 'This family is dealing with more than enough irregularity at present.'

'Of course, ma'am. I do not wish to

add to your difficulties.'

'I think a Christmas wedding will be a delight to look forward to in the darker days. Many of the family will be in Town.' Lady Mellon looked round the small group, and Daisy watched heads nod in agreement. Her mama's pronouncements rarely elicited any other reaction, of course, but Daisy knew Reuben Longreach liked to stir matters that were moving along smoothly. And once again he proved her right.

'Some of us are already in Town,' he said.

'Indeed you are, Reuben. What is it that justifies your continued absence from the family estate?' Lady Mellon asked.

'Why, the estate is small, ma'am, and goes along under the reins of my steward, giving little trouble to any of us.' Reuben winked at her, and Daisy sighed. It was well known in the family that her cousin was regarded by the mamas of rural Hampshire as a prime candidate for marriage. He, however, seemed increasingly reluctant to find himself a betrothed, and in order to escape, frequently trespassed on the earl's hospitality.

'Stop teasing Mama, Reuben. Perhaps you would help some of the ladies to the champagne Stephens is handing round.' Toby brought them all back to the business of the day. There was a betrothal to mark, and the butler had organised glasses of the sparkling wine which he and a footman were now offering the assembled family.

'Daisy, I could not wish for a better husband for you,' Toby said. 'John, my sister will make you a most fitting wife. I propose a toast of happiness and long life together for Daisy and John.' He smiled at them both as he raised his glass in a salute.

Daisy felt tears threaten and covered her confusion by dropping her head modestly. It was all very well to rail against the behaviour of her relatives, but they did love her, and she was touched by their happiness over her betrothal.

* * *

During the afternoon, Daisy found herself alone in the library with Reuben. John had gone off to his house at Richmond to tell his sisters, Amelia, Jayne and Elizabeth, of his betrothal and to continue his convalescence. Toby was once more attending the law officers, and Lady Mellon was writing some of the many letters the betrothal had necessitated.

'Your mama has not asked you to write on her behalf?' Reuben asked as Daisy sighed for the umpteenth time. She felt his careful gaze rake her features. Did this man have sterling qualities? Daisy sometimes thought she could see behind his mask of insouciance to a different individual. It was puzzling and unsettling. She returned his gaze with a cool stare.

'You know perfectly well Mama does not trust me to commit enough gravity to the task of telling dowager aunts and impoverished cousins I am to be married to a coal baron,' she said. She watched Reuben struggle to school his expression and fail. His bark of laughter was a cheering sound in the huge room lined with her late papa's collection of books and maps.

'Will there be much disappointment?'

'Much. My inheritance has been actively sought by three cousins, who will be desolate. On the other hand, at least two aunts will feel I should have passed up the opportunity of diluting the blood line with coal dust.' Daisy rose and swept across the rugs to gaze out onto a wet and dismal back garden. 'It was so hot earlier. I do hope these thunderstorms will retreat and allow us to walk out again.'

'Properly clad, you could walk out now. Has your indisposition sufficiently left you?' Reuben joined her at the windows. 'I would be glad to escort you to Hatchard's bookshop if you wanted to buy a new novel.'

The offer was too tempting to resist, and within twenty minutes, Reuben, Daisy and her maid Smithers were walking along Grosvenor Square. Daisy kept her hand tucked into Reuben's arm. She had suffered greatly from the bad shellfish eaten at an evening party and her head was still occasionally light. They reached the bookshop on Piccadilly and strolled through the tables and shelves. Reuben paused over a volume of mathematics and Daisy kept moving slowly along. She had a mind to buy something for John to mark their betrothal, and was about to ask an assistant where she could view some of Walter Scott's recent work, when a voice she had no wish to encounter spoke.

2

'Daisy,' Amarinta Wellwood said, with a slight catch betraying nervousness.

It is as if she does not expect me to acknowledge her, Daisy thought. She cast a glance around the shop floor and realised Amarinta stood alone, although there were several other young matrons and females of their circle present.

'Good afternoon, Amarinta,' Daisy replied. She felt the rustle of her skirts caused by Smithers moving close behind her and turned to the girl. 'Thank you, Smithers.' Daisy waited while her maid moved out of hearing before she addressed Amarinta again. 'What can you possibly have to say to me?'

'So much — and yet, as you suggest, nothing at all,' the other girl said with diffidence she had never previously shown. 'I am now married to Mr Reginald Barlow. As you know, he had secured a special licence, and we went ahead with the ceremony, despite Lucas's death. I leave for the north very soon.'

Daisy did not know about the special licence and again inwardly railed against her brother for keeping things from her. There was no need for Amarinta to learn that, however, and she acknowledged the little speech with a slight nod.

'Reginald rescued me from an encounter with Lucas the day he died, and I have since wondered whether my abrupt departure was responsible for his death.' The young woman dipped her head and Daisy could not see her distinctive green eyes, but she sounded genuinely distressed.

'Rescued you?' she asked, startled by the choice of word. 'Why did you require rescuing from Lucas? He was always the most attentive of guardians.'

'That is very kind of you, Daisy, but I know Mariah Fox will have told you of our meeting that day, and . . .' Amarinta stopped speaking and passed her tiny gloved hand along the spines of the books she was holding. 'Suffice it to say, Miss Fox was not wrong in her assessment. She is a formidable force and will make Tobias a worthy countess. I would be indebted if you were to pass on to her my warm felicitations, as I will likely not see her again.'

Daisy smiled, as much in desperation as anything else, but it had the desired effect on her former friend, who kept talking.

'I have been solicited by the law officers to appear before them, Daisy.' She cast a glance toward a group of older ladies who watched them like vultures from across the room. Her feet shuffled, but she grasped a little composure and continued. 'Lady Barlow, Reginald's mama, is against it, as she believes it will only inflame the gossip already surrounding Lucas's death. Now I am dependent on her goodwill, I must consider her opinion.'

'And yet, did not Mariah and Toby set out to rescue you from a parlous existence?' Daisy shot in the dark, basing her question on the snippets she had gleaned.

Certainly Mariah had no obvious business being at Ogle Road where Wellwood had his lodgings. Was it not a possibility she had gone on a mission to seek out Amarinta? she wondered.

Amarinta's head snapped up. The green eyes flooded with tears as she focused on Daisy. 'Daisy, you show me my duty. Lucas was evil. I will collect Perkins and insist Reginald take us to the law officers. It is all I can do to make reparations, and I will do it.'

'Perkins?' Daisy was confused. The only Perkins she could think of was Toby's valet, and he had never worked for the Wellwoods.

'Yes, Rodney Perkins. He used to be a footman in Mama's household. His younger brother works for the earl, and he approached Rodney. That prompted Rodney to come to me for advice. There was an incident while he was still in Mama's employ, a parlour maid … found dead, at the bottom of the stairs. It's very likely she did not fall down the stairwell, but was thrown down. She had bruising on her arms and her dress was ripped.' Amarinta leant forward and kissed Daisy quickly on the cheek. 'Goodbye, Daisy.'

Daisy stood for a few seconds after Amarinta dropped her books and dashed from the shop. She remembered John's cryptic remark about a parlour maid, and was beginning to make sense of the mess the men found themselves in over Wellwood's death. It began to look as if Mariah had worked out that Wellwood would harm Amarinta, perhaps in the face of her failure to secure Toby's hand, and had gone to rescue her.

She thought of all the hushed conversations taking place around the house in Grosvenor Square and picked out tiny morsels of information. Toby was exasperated with his future wife but relieved she had survived *unscathed*. Perkins was as nervous as a cat, Smithers reported.

'What sort of rocket did you put under your friend? She's the new Mrs Barlow, I believe,' Reuben spoke at her elbow. 'She's left in more than a hurry.'

'She has, has she not?' Daisy replied.

The moment had come to demonstrate she, too, could keep secrets. Besides, as a hopeful writer of alarming fictions, she had much to think over. Life going on around her was proving to be much richer with possibility than anything she had so far thought up by herself. 'Now, Reuben, I wish to purchase some volumes of Walter Scott to present to John.'

'As a betrothal gift?' Reuben asked without missing a beat, but Daisy was not fooled. He would pursue the information from her in his own ways, and it would be a considerable challenge to keep it from him. The kind of challenge she did not envisage as John's wife.

Oh, will I miss Reuben when I am no longer able to engage with him as freely?

'Yes,' she answered. 'While I am sure his prose is worth much praise, in this instance it's the quality of the bindings that make the works attractive to me.'

'The love of your life is not an intellectual then?'

Daisy surveyed her companion, but his slightly lifted eyebrow proved her undoing. She tried hard to stifle a nervous giggle. 'John is much interested in engineering matters, but he likes to dress the shelves of his library appropriately.'

* * *

The family party which assembled around the smaller dining room table that evening was jubilant.

'Tobias, I am much relieved by this news,' Lady Mellon said for at least the third time since her son had returned from the law officers. 'And Amarinta Wellwood came to them of her own free will?'

'Not exactly, Mama. She had been solicited on two occasions, but declined. Something may have happened to change her mind.' Tobias's glance came sideways, but Daisy was ready for him and did not drop her gaze. She was enjoying the small thrill of secretly knowing that her words to Amarinta had made a difference to the outcome of Toby's case.

'This is the young woman you met

in Hatchard's today,' Reuben said, as if discovering the connection for the first time. Daisy decided she would have to agree.

'Yes. She is now Mrs Barlow, Mama. They were married by special licence, despite Lucas's death. She must have had a busy day if she was shopping in Hatchard's but also addressing the law officers,' Daisy said, and did not look in Reuben's direction.

'I am surprised she had the effrontery to address you in a public place,' huffed Aunt Mathilde, saying what everyone else was thinking.

'No one else approached her. I did not either,' Daisy said fairly. 'But I was unable to cut her. We have been friends, you know.'

'When will your case be finally settled, Tobias?' Lady Mellon toyed with some turtle soup. She had ordered a special dinner to mark Daisy's betrothal and the near-certain favourable outcome of Tobias's inquisition, but Daisy saw she was not eating much of it. The nervous exhaustion caused by all the upheavals was taking a toll on her.

'Some further days are needed while the law clerks write up the dispositions and such other formalities. It will all be over in time for the wedding.' Toby spoke reassuringly to their mother, and Daisy welled with pride in her brother. Although the earldom had not been his birthright, Toby filled the role with easy assurance and was very kind to his relatives. Even now, Aunt Mathilde leaned across the space between them and patted his hand. How many earls permitted such familiarity?

'You have come through, Tobias,' the old lady said. 'And your lady has proved she will be a fitting countess.'

Daisy flushed. Mariah, if she'd done what Daisy now suspected and gone off to Wellwood's lodgings with some scatterbrained idea of persuading him to leave aside his plans, had put several lives at risk. Toby, John, her maid, Tilly, and several of Toby's male friends had been endangered. Countesses might show a little forethought, she felt.

'One wonders what persuaded the lady to go rushing into the lion's den,' Reuben observed to no one in particular. 'I hope she learns to hesitate.'

'Really,' Tobias said in the clipped tones Daisy knew only too well. They inevitably preceded a formidable set-down, and even, when she was still a schoolroom miss, a swat on the derrière. 'You need not concern yourself over the future countess's behaviour. She will be more than equal to upholding the family name.'

'No doubt, sir, but will you be comfortable?'

'Comfortable? Miss Fox's intellect ensures life will never be comfortable again, but I look forward to the challenge.' Tobias turned away to ask Lady Mellon which other relatives were making the trip from Scotland for his wedding.

'You are studying me with an expression of deep irritation, Daisy,' Reuben said a few seconds later. The conversation around the table had broken up into groups following the earl's example, and they were free to speak without being much attended.

'And why not, sir? Has my brother not got enough trouble worrying him without your sly remarks about Mariah's behaviour?' Daisy spoke with more warmth than she intended, because Reuben had voiced the thoughts she'd been nursing too.

'I think, ma'am, that guilt makes you rather fierce.' Reuben raised an eyebrow.

'What can you mean? Everyone is now speaking of how brave Mariah was to beard that monster in his home,' she protested.

'Perhaps, but I think Tobias would have preferred her to restrain her impulses.' The infuriating man moved his knife around on the cloth, and Daisy's eyes were drawn to the elegance of his fingers. He played several instruments rather well. There was always music in the air when Reuben stayed with them.

'It is resolved, though,' she said. 'The world is no doubt better without Lucas Wellwood, and his sister in particular is safer.' She stopped, aware she'd been about to tell Reuben the information she'd been withholding so well.

'That is why the lady has gone to the law officers, I've no doubt. You made her realise what she owed to Tobias and Mariah.' Reuben smiled. He looked pleased he'd prised the information from her. 'Clever girl.'

Daisy smarted under his remark. 'It wasn't perhaps as brave as fighting a kidnap gang and suspected murderer, but it does seem to have taken the trick,' she said.

'You are the most beautiful woman of my acquaintance when you are angry, Daisy Mellon.'

'Reuben!' she protested. 'You have no business talking to me in this manner.'

'Of course not,' he agreed easily. She could see he was seeking to take the wind out of her sails. 'We are cousins, however, and you may excuse me on those grounds alone.'

'We are not very near cousins, and if

you repeat any such sentiments, I will be obliged to tell Mama, sir.'

* * *

Daisy sat on after Smithers had undressed her for bed. She went to the window and eased her shutters open so the back garden was visible below her in uncertain moonlight. Clouds scudded across the sky, obscuring the moon and plunging everything outside into darkness from moment to moment. A figure moved below. Smoke curled up, and Daisy realised it was someone from the household taking the air. As if alerted to her presence, he turned.

Reuben! She stepped back into the shadow of her curtains, but he had seen the movement against what must be a faint light from her remaining candles.

'Come down and join me,' he called in a stage whisper. 'The library door is open.'

She clipped the shutters and stepped into the middle of her room. Typical Reuben. Did he think they were still in the schoolroom? That unmarried ladies, recently betrothed, could wander in the moonlight with not-very-near cousins? Her thoughts chased each other in their haste to persuade her it would be a very bad idea indeed to go down to the darkened garden.

She paced. Life was so stultifying. She no longer even had her feud with John to keep her brain stimulated. He'd found an answer to their problem. The sour moment of disappointment rose in her memory to torment her.

The library door was open and she slipped out onto the flagstones. A hand tapped her on the shoulder and she barely suppressed a squeal of fright.

'Your nervous reaction makes me think again of a guilty conscience, Daisy Mellon.' Reuben linked arms with her and led her to a stout bench under a lime tree. 'Tobias will not be surprised to find you out here, should he come wandering. It was a great shock to see the extent of John Brent's injuries for the first time, I'm sure.'

'Yes, it was. Had you seen him since the fight?'

Reuben nodded.

'Yet you didn't think to warn me? I could have gone to Richmond to nurture him.'

'Exactly. You must know Tobias and your mama worked very hard to prevent John coming here, or to give you reason to visit him there. I would have been lacking all the graces of a guest if I had gone against their wishes. And yet, I did warn you this morning when his visit was a certainty.' He withdrew his arm and settled back against the bench with one leg crossed over the other at the knee.

Daisy watched the muscles ripple through the thin material of his evening pantaloons. He was an artistic individual, but he was also a good horseman, and when in Town went often to Mr Jackson's rooms to spar. John was an indifferent horseman and would only ever be in Mr Jackson's rooms to meet a friend.

She opened her eyes wide. Where did these disloyal thoughts have their origin?

She stood up. It had been some kind of midsummer madness to come out here in her bed-gown and a wrapper.

Reuben rose fluidly at her side, and she sensed his watchfulness more acutely than ever. What did he want from her?

'You are as scratchy as a kitten tonight, Daisy. Let's walk round the garden. The rains have refreshed everything and lifted scent into the air.' As he spoke, Reuben linked arms with her again, and Daisy found herself walking along the central path.

'We can be seen by anyone looking out as I was looking earlier,' she murmured.

'Of course,' her escort replied, and added with maddening sense, 'If we were hugging the paths around the walls, they might think we were involved in a tryst, but as we walk the central path, all must be innocent cousinly companionship.'

Daisy digested this before replying, 'Would you be interested in meeting me for a tryst? Only, I think you should make it known soon, as our Scottish cousin, Miss Elspeth Howie, must surely be looking for a husband, and she arrives here tomorrow.'

Reuben laughed, and like the thunder of earlier in the day, it cleared her head. 'Of course not, silly child. If I had wanted to secure your attentions, I could have done so long since. You and Mr Brent were more often to be found squabbling than making love. Given it was his unavailability that was his main attraction, I should simply have caused the earl to forbid you my acquaintance.'

'That's nonsensical.'

'Do not fool yourself over the earl's keen eye for the suitable, my dear,' Reuben interrupted her. 'He has firm views on acceptability. I find myself wondering whether John Brent was the more attractive to you because you are used to men fawning over you.'

'Fawning over my inheritance, more like.' Her joy in this illicit encounter was ebbing away. Reuben had brought her down here for a reason.

'It is indeed substantial, but any man would know how difficult life would be if he brought you no more than gambling debts and impecunious relatives.' Reuben held her arm tightly when she tried to draw away. 'No, little one, don't squirm. Mr Brent is an honourable man, but should he not prove to be the love of your life, then act bravely.'

'Reuben!'

'Perhaps Tobias is too preoccupied to say these things to you, but I think someone must.'

'You presume too much on our childhood companionship, sir. Goodnight.'

Daisy left him and went back to her room. The hem of her bed-gown was wet, so she stripped it off and climbed into the bed naked. The sheets were cool against her skin, and she stretched like the kitten Reuben had likened her to, revelling in sensation she had never previously experienced.

Would John meet her in their garden in the moonlight? She knew, of course, that youngish widows and some matrons would sneak out of balls to secret rendezvous in the grounds of great houses, but she was uncertain what they did there. Just as she was uncertain what John would do on their wedding night. Daisy wriggled. The linen smelled of lavender. No doubt Mama would tell her what she might expect when John came to her. If circumstances had been different, she could have asked Amarinta.

As the last candle in her room guttered and died, she heard Reuben's words again in her head. *'It was Brent's unavailability that was his main attraction.'*

Was there ever such a provoking man?

3

'Lady Daisy,' a Scottish voice carried across the tiled lower hall. It was attractive and brought a smile to Daisy's eyes even as she raised her head to face her visitor. 'Mama and Grandmamma are dearly looking forward to renewing their acquaintance with you.'

Daisy hesitated before stepping off the staircase she'd been descending and crossing to her relative, Miss Elspeth Howie. The girl was at least two years older than Daisy, possibly three. She had her hair secured beneath a battered hat with fraying ribbons and wore a travelling costume of thick Scottish tweed in an indeterminate colour. The ensemble contrived to made her look at least thirty.

'Cousin Elspeth,' Daisy said. She shrugged off the shock of her cousin's bedraggled appearance and would have embraced her, but for the number and volume of items Elspeth was holding, carrying, or dropping.

'Stephens, can someone assist Miss Howie?'

'Don't worry about me, Lady Daisy,' the girl said, but relinquished a leather grip, two books, a stone hot-water pig, and a paper wrapper that looked to hold the remains of some bread, when the butler came closer. Stephens transferred the haul to a footman. She heard a step coming smartly along the garden passage behind her, and saw the smile light Elspeth's violet eyes when she recognised Reuben.

'Why, it's cousin Reuben.' Elspeth unwound a shawl from her shoulders and another from around her waist. She allowed a maid to catch them as they slid floorwards. 'I didn't know you were staying, too.'

Reuben surged forward and enveloped Elspeth. Daisy, surprised by this show of intimacy, stepped aside. When had they met? she wondered. How had they come to know each other so well that a polite bow and curtsey was bypassed in favour of this warmth?

'I have been staying, but am now ejected in favour of you invading Scots,' Reuben said with just enough lightness of tone to take the sting from his remark. 'My mama and my aunts will be arriving on the morrow to stay in most respectable lodgings nearby. As you can imagine only too well, they will be in need of my assistance.'

Elspeth cast Reuben the kind of glance Daisy's mama would have called old-fashioned, had she been here to greet her guests rather than shut away in her room with a crippling headache. Was there something about Elspeth's standing in the life of her family she did not know, but Reuben did?

'Where are the other members of your party, Elspeth?' Daisy asked. The girl looked much slimmer since she'd been divested of the extra layers of tweed. There was nothing to redeem the woeful travelling costume, however, and Daisy wondered what the remainder of her relative's wardrobe was going to contain.

'Papa dropped off to sleep about an hour ago, and Mama thought it best if I came in ahead of the party while they collect themselves. Grandmamma dotes on him, of course, and encourages Mama to ensure he is not unduly travailed by the difficulties of travelling,' Elspeth said. 'Even if Conor is the very best coachman and has brought us south with such ease.' The girl dropped her head while she toyed with a loose button on the front of her jacket. Daisy watched as Reuben covered her fingers with his and brought her hand through his arm, and was surprised by a shaft of what could be construed as jealousy.

'My dear Elspeth,' he said, 'Daisy will ensure they are safely decanted from their coach and the estimable Conor directed to the mews. Come with me into the breakfast parlour, where I know Mrs Burtles has had chocolate and cold cuts sent in for your arrival.' Reuben would have begun to walk toward the parlour, but Elspeth stayed him.

'Reuben, I cannot leave Lady Daisy to deal with my family on her own,' she protested, and Daisy saw a tiny flare of pink flush the other girl's cheeks. 'You know from your visit to us last autumn how very difficult they can be when tired.'

'I do know how very difficult they can be, and I assure you Lady Daisy and her maid, who was brought up in the Foundling Hospital, will be more than a match for their foibles.'

'Reuben,' the lady exclaimed, but it was no use. Daisy knew Reuben of old. He had insulted Miss Howie's parents and grandmamma while every syllable was pitched at civility, but he was not going to give way to the young lady's sensibilities. She was to be cosseted and Daisy was to stand in for her.

'How difficult can it be, Elspeth?' Daisy asked equably enough, but she was angry with Reuben for placing her in this position. 'My aunt and uncle and Mrs Howie must surely be looking forward to the visit and Toby's wedding.'

'One would think so,' Elspeth said, with so little conviction that Daisy quailed.

* * *

'I will not easily forgive you, Reuben,' Daisy said later in the day when they sat out in the garden sipping cold cordials. Her Scottish relatives, the first wave of house-guests for Toby's marriage, had at last been installed in rooms to their satisfaction. She was bruised by their volley of complaints and impertinence. 'No wonder Elspeth looks to be at her last prayers.'

'Unkind, Daisy,' Reuben said without raising his voice. 'Having experienced her parents and grandmother for two hours, you can surely understand why I wished to offer her a little respite.' He glanced at her and Daisy knew she blushed under the scrutiny. 'Gawd, they were awful when I stayed in their house on Edinburgh's Queen Street. It rises through five floors and Elspeth is confined in an attic room, on the same floor with the maids.'

'Why would they wish my cousin to sleep among the staff?' Daisy was puzzled by Reuben's assertion. 'My aunt was most particular about the family being allocated a suite commensurate with their status. It was almost as if she thought I did not remember she was Papa's sister.'

'There was a certain disappointment when Leo died, as Lady Beatrice had been promoting an alliance between Elspeth and the earl.' Reuben stood, and carrying his glass, paced a little. 'Elspeth refused to exert herself to capture his successor.'

'Toby? My aunt thought to arrange a marriage between Elspeth Howie and the heir — whoever the heir might be?'

'Your understanding is quick this afternoon.'

'Do not use such a patronising tone when speaking to me, Reuben. I was in the schoolroom when Leo died. Thereafter, Toby has not shared his matrimonial intentions with me.'

'No, that would be why you felt able to promote Miss Wellwood's suit,' he surmised.

'I think, sir, it would be as well were you to remove your person to those most respectable lodgings you mentioned before I ask Stephens to eject you,' Daisy said.

'You are white with fury, my dear. Have I trodden on your sensibilities?' Reuben asked without compunction.

Daisy hated him in that moment. 'I did not promote Amarinta Wellwood's pursuit of Toby, but Lady Mellon did. She now regrets it bitterly, and I would be most grateful if you would keep your thrilling discoveries to yourself.' Daisy snapped out the words without thought. Giving Reuben information of that kind was asking for trouble.

'Your mama has suffered from this sort of headache before, Daisy. She will recover.' Reuben touched on Daisy's real anxiety with his usual precision. He stretched. She watched the supple length of him. He had shown such care of Elspeth earlier, and now that she'd seen the unreasonable behaviour of her relatives she understood why, but she still resented it.

'You are right to relate Mama's headache to the recent events. She's been sick, and her companion reports she sees flashing lights.' She stood, and would have motioned for a footman to show Reuben out, but her cousin stayed her hand.

'A moment, Daisy, if you please.'

Reuben's hand on her arm sent a frisson of heat along it. He was standing so close she could see the flecks of gold in his irises. She could smell his soap and the lingering aroma of his tobacco. He was altogether too close, and too masculine.

'I see much that others are unaware of. I see that our cousin Elspeth is being ground down by her failure to do as her family wished, and I would make her visit as cheerful as possible. Will you help?'

'It is my duty to help Mama make all our guests comfortable, and —'

'Daisy! Will you help me set Elspeth Howie back on her feet?'

Daisy regarded Reuben with fresh insight. Did he have a particular reason for wanting to help Elspeth? Was it his intention to make sure she secured a bridegroom? The earl may be spoken for, but he was unattached.

Or did he not realise what an excellent bride Elspeth would make for him? Daisy caught her tongue between her teeth lest she make a squeal of satisfaction.

Reuben had a small estate and a regular income from it. He was well able to support a bride. She suppressed a smile. A little intrigue would be a great help in lessening the impact of her relatives' extended visit.

'I will certainly help all I can,' she said.

* * *

Reuben leapt from step to step, off the staircase and onto the pavement outside the earl's magnificent townhouse. He picked up a brisk pace and headed towards the lodgings where he was booked to stay for the next three weeks or so with his mama, younger sister Charlotte, and aunts. As he walked, he reflected on a good morning's work.

Daisy was thoroughly unsettled by her experience with her aunt and uncle and Mrs Howie. She had coped with Lady Mellon's fits of temper for many years, of course, but that lady was also rational and not given to contrariness such as the visitors had shown. Reuben had heard their increasingly obdurate demands echo round the halls and stairwells as Daisy and Mrs Burtles tried to find rooms fulfilling all their wishes.

Across the corner of the breakfast parlour table, Elspeth had become paler and paler until those amazing violet eyes filled her face. Reuben poured more steaming chocolate into her cup, heaped pastries onto her plate, and filled a small bowl with strawberries.

'Reuben, they will not be happy until they know I've been allocated the smallest guest bedroom available, with the assurance I'll be removed should any other relative require it,' she'd said without heat or self-pity. The very calmness of her words fired something in Reuben's blood, and he determined she would not leave London without the protection of a husband's name.

'Your grandmamma may very well dictate where you sleep in her son's house, but in this house, Lady Mellon will not be coerced into playing her games.'

'You underestimate her determination.' Elspeth tucked a stray lock of night-black hair behind her ear and smiled at him. 'She will go to her grave believing I could have been the next Countess of Mellon.'

'Have events been a disappointment to you, my dear?'

'I was very sad when Leo died, but in truth I think he only agreed to visit us that time because he was lacking in other occupation,' Elspeth said. 'He never offered for me. My relatives were plotting a return visit to further his suit, which in my mind did not exist, when the news came.'

'And then Tobias?' Reuben kept his gaze neutral, but he was watching his cousin closely. Any young woman would find Toby a more attractive prospect than his older brother had been.

'Tobias?' Elspeth reflected for a moment or two. 'I have seen the way some of my friends go on in their marriages, Reuben. With a man like Tobias it would be very good, I think, for perhaps a year or two. He is civil and well-meaning; but forced into a dynastic marriage, I am convinced he would be suffocated. It would be very lowering to know your husband sought his mental stimulation elsewhere. I could not bear that.'

Reuben was startled by this frank assessment of the married state. He began to understand why Elspeth's parents were reacting the way they were. She was no schoolroom chit to be fobbed off with the pretence that her parents knew best, but a woman of decided views. It also gave him a clue about her banishment to the attics in Edinburgh. With such perspicacity, Elspeth Howie would pick up on everything around her. He knew there were things her relatives did not want her to pick up on.

'I wish Miss Fox warm felicitations. I am convinced she will earn every ruby Tobias places round her neck.'

Elspeth Howie was bright, beautiful, and ripe for the hand of a suitable male.

Reuben turned into the doorway of his lodgings and chuckled as he remembered her words, delivered with a thrust of a determined chin. No, his Scots cousin was not wasting away for love of a Countess's title. She was, however, wasting away in the service of two mean-spirited women and a weak-willed papa. The ground for mischief-making was well tilled.

4

Daisy sat at the bottom of a formal table opposite Toby. Ranked along the sides were her newly arrived relatives from Edinburgh and two other families from the north. Aunt Mathilde sat at Toby's right hand, displacing and displeasing her aunt, Lady Beatrice, who was on his left. Despite the coolness of their parting earlier, she was very relieved Reuben had returned to the house for dinner.

'I thought I would chance my luck while your mama keeps to her room,' he said when Stephens announced him. 'Toby might be glad of some younger blood after the ladies depart the dining room.'

'I cannot fault your thinking, sir, but I am fast coming to Mama's view of your life and wonder how your estate can spare you for such long periods.'

'Nonsense, Daisy. I am here to play at

several concerts which will benefit the Foundling Hospital. It was all arranged many months since. It's the spate of weddings that is freakish.' He'd accepted a glass of champagne from a footman and raised it in mock salute.

Now he sat three places from her, and she could not always hear the words he directed to Elspeth seated by him. Elspeth's papa, Mr Howie, was a man of little conversation, but he did breathe heavily. Sitting at Daisy's right, he set up a considerable barrier between her and the guests on that length of the table.

'Daisy!' Her aunt's peremptory tones interrupted her wool-gathering. What had Aunt Beatrice said? Daisy wondered. She would have to ask her to repeat it, because she would be ill-advised to agree or disagree with anything the woman said without knowing the facts.

'Ma'am?'

'I am relieved indeed to discover I am not a ghost, niece.' Her aunt's stridency would be envied by any ghost hoping to instil fear and trembling in a company,

Daisy reflected.

'I do beg your pardon, Aunt Beatrice. I was momentarily distracted, remembering the poignant words Elspeth used earlier about my papa's sense of fairness and social justice,' she said, hoping to divert the mama by praise of her child. However, Aunt Beatrice was not a naturally inclined parent.

'Elspeth on occasion offers her opinions where a young lady of breeding, such as she has had every opportunity of becoming, would keep quiet,' Aunt Beatrice said loudly enough to bring other conversations to a standstill. 'I don't doubt the future countess has been chosen because she fulfils all the criteria your mama thought necessary in one who would replace her — and my own dear departed mama.'

The words were directed at Toby, and Daisy dug her nails into her palms. She saw the quick angry flush darken her brother's face and caught sight of Reuben's fingers falling below the board. No doubt he was clasping Elspeth's hand in reassurance, and Daisy envied the other girl in that moment. When would John be well enough to return, that she might be supported, too?

'Why, I have chosen Miss Fox for the strength of her opinions and the unfaltering nature of her beliefs,' Toby said. 'I haven't seen much of her for several days due to a little unpleasantness I've been obliged to deal with, but should Mama be on her feet again tomorrow, I will be rectifying that omission.'

Daisy knew her aunt hadn't been in company with Toby since he was a green and untried youth, but anyone of the least sensibility would hear the warning in his tone — anyone except her aunt.

'Are you telling me Constanzia has permitted your betrothal to a —'

'No, Aunt. The only permission I required was from Mr Fox to address his daughter, and thereafter Miss Fox and I have made our own arrangements.'

Daisy saw the glance full of anguish Toby sent toward her, and she looked round to attract Stephens's attention.

Within seconds, the butler had footmen removing plates and laying down clean ones. It was impossible for a general conversation to continue.

* * *

The following morning was enlivened by a visit from John Brent. Daisy was so pleased to see him, she had to restrain the impulse to throw herself into his arms and thereby further damage his cracked ribs.

'John, my love,' she said warmly as he entered the morning parlour where Daisy presided, in her mama's continued absence, over a reduced gathering of relatives. Several had gone off to explore the warehouses and make visits to milliners and modistes. Daisy wondered uncharitably whether the presence of her aunt had sent them scurrying out, when they had all travelled considerable distances yesterday and might have wished to spend the day more lazily.

'John, Mama is recovering from one of

her sick headaches but hopes to be well enough to join us for dinner this evening. Are you able to stay on, or do the Misses Brent need you back in Richmond?' Daisy had introduced John to her aunt, Lady Beatrice, and the others. Now she found herself almost begging him to stay. Even if her mama was well enough to come down, her recovery would not be helped by sparring with Aunt Beatrice. While Daisy could think of many excellent put-downs, she knew they would come back to snap at her heels in due course.

'Fortunately, Daisy, my love, I am at your disposal for several days. If a bed can be found in a corner of the house, I am minded to continue my convalescence here.' The words were ponderous, but the sparkle of mischief in John's eyes had a lot to do with his first encounter with Lady Beatrice and her mama-in-law, Mrs Howie. Daisy hesitated. She knew how much her betrothed enjoyed the cut and thrust of social politics, and too late, realised she could by no means trust him to behave. She wondered whether he was not already plotting how best to upset and undermine the dreadful Mrs Howie.

'That is very good news, my love. However, I wonder whether Mrs Burtles does have a bed comfortable enough to assist the healing of your injuries.'

'Nonsense, niece. I'm sure the bed you assigned to Elspeth would be most suitable for Mr Brent's recovery. I shall make sure Burtles moves Elspeth's belongings forthwith. There are always some of those small attic rooms unallocated,' Lady Beatrice said.

Daisy gripped her skirts so tightly she felt a seam give way between her fingers.

What would Mama do in these circumstances?

Seconds ticked on as silence born of embarrassment collected in the room, making it as unstable as a powder keg. The great Louis Quatorze clock on the mantelpiece chimed the quarter and woke Daisy from her paralysis. How dare her aunt threaten her position as her mama's depute?

'Aunt Beatrice, I do appreciate your

concern for the family's guests, but you must not feel under any pressure to take up housekeeping duties. Mrs Burtles and I will manage until Mama is restored to health.' She crossed to the fireplace and rang the service bell. 'Besides, I know Toby will want John to use one of the rooms in his wing, as he is to be his supporter at the marriage next week.'

Daisy watched the flush rise on John's cheeks as he darted a glance at Elspeth. He was clearly mortified at any suggestion a lady, and moreover a lady who was one of the family, should be ousted from her comforts on his behalf.

'Lady Beatrice,' John said, 'I would never permit Miss Howie to be dislodged from her accommodation for my comfort. You cannot think it.'

'Why, sir, Elspeth has to realise how little importance is attached to the granddaughter of an earl when the young person has done nothing to improve her position in life,' Mrs Howie intervened, huffing the words with decided irritation, and Daisy was relieved to see the door open to admit Stephens.

'M'lady?' the butler asked.

'Mr Brent will be staying with us for a few days, Stephens. Would you ask Mrs Burtles to make ready one of the rooms in the earl's private quarters, please?'

'Of course, m'lady. Mr Reuben has arrived, m'lady, and wonders if he may attend you.'

'Show him in,' Daisy said. Surely he could not make matters any worse, she thought.

'Lady Daisy,' Reuben said when he entered a moment or two later. He bowed over her hand, and with a steely glint in his eye only she could see, lifted her fingers to his lips. She snatched her hand away as if he'd nipped it with the strong teeth in his gleaming smile. His eyebrows raised a fraction. Daisy stepped forward and, stumbling, trod on Reuben's foot.

'My apologies, sir. I had not realised you were standing so close.'

Daisy sat down and her aunt reluctantly followed suit, allowing both young men to take seats. John crossed to the sofa occupied by Elspeth and dropped beside her. Reuben, who had begun to walk toward the lady, settled instead beside Aunt Mathilde. Daisy realised he had an excellent view of the whole room and all its occupants from there. She sent up a prayer for her mama's instant recovery.

* * *

My, my, she's in a taking. The aunt looks as if she's sucking on a lemon, and if the old lady purses her lips any harder they'll disappear into her mouth.

Reuben gathered his thoughts as he allowed his gaze to roam over the room's occupants. It was annoying to him that Brent had taken a seat beside Elspeth, but on the other hand, perhaps it was to the good. The young lady now had two gentlemen below the age of senility prepared to talk to her.

What has gone forward? I wonder. Elspeth was such a high colour when I came in, but she is calming down now.

Brent is embarrassed. Aunt Mathilde is on her mettle to defend Daisy, I can see. Mr Howie snores. And Lady Beatrice ...

'I am surprised my sister-in-law makes you quite as welcome as you obviously feel you are, Mr Longreach,' Lady Beatrice said, interrupting Reuben's satisfying perusal of the room's occupants. 'But then extra gentlemen are very useful in the evening.'

'Why, and so I can be, ma'am. However, I am in London for reasons other than the wedding of the earl, you know.' Reuben smiled reassuringly at Elspeth, whose beautiful eyes were clouded with confusion and embarrassment. How appalling it must be to know one's mama was the daughter of an earl but had inherited only the manners of a partly civilised savage with little education.

'Other reasons? What other reasons?'

'You are awake, sir.' Reuben addressed Mr Howie, who had sprung suddenly to life. 'I am playing a series of concerts, organ recitals in fact, at the request of the organising council of the Foundling Hospital.'

'Those people,' Lady Beatrice snapped. 'How much money this family has poured into their funds over the years, I shudder to compute.'

'You compute, ma'am? I had thought you disdained any such activity lest it turn into nervous affliction,' Reuben said, causing John Brent to choke back a shout of laughter by pretending it was a cough.

'Mama,' Elspeth protested, and Reuben thought she must be sorely provoked to draw her mama's attention to her. 'You know Uncle Frederick was a devoted supporter of the hospital.'

'Of course I know that, Elspeth. My brother was always taking on staff from their numbers and advising the rest of us to do so, but what is the point? If these people are the children of feckless women who were unable to support their children, why should we expect those children to be any better a prospect?'

'You believe poverty is the fault of a wronged woman, Lady Beatrice?'

'My wife has strong principles, sir. Organ recitals, eh? I had thought you knew of something more masculine.' Mr Howie made his longest speech of his visit so far. 'A mill, perhaps? You make a good showing at Jackson's rooms, don't ye?'

'I go there for the exercise from time to time, but I need to take care not to injure my hands, so I am not perhaps as good as others who have no such constraints,' Reuben replied. He knew Mr Howie would be little interested in any of the parties or other events arranged to mark the earl's marriage. 'I am not aware of any prize fights taking place while you are with the earl.'

'Pity,' Mr Howie allowed before dropping his head onto his chest again and going back to sleep.

Reuben was aware of the ladies shifting around him. They moved their feet and smoothed the material of their dresses like so many hens in a coop. Lady Mellon would find her work cut out when she recovered her health. Although Daisy was trying valiantly, her aunt was an expert in creating unhappiness. Reuben knew it was time to act.

'I saw your carriage being led off, Mr Brent. Would it be available should we decide to take the air?'

John Brent cast Reuben a sorry glance before replying, 'To tell you truly, Longreach, I'd as soon walk out, if the young ladies did not object. My injuries, you understand, make coach travel deuced uncomfortable ...'

Reuben was instantly contrite. 'I do beg your pardon, Brent. The repercussions from that sorry event seem to go on and on. However, I think a walk as far as the Grosvenor Chapel would be beneficial to the young ladies. Daisy, can the redoubtable Burtles spare you until luncheon?'

The effect on Daisy was all Reuben might have hoped and more. She threw him a generous smile and nodded, but the euphoria of the moment was spoiled by Lady Beatrice.

'I hope you do not intend to set in motion the idle habits you encouraged in Elspeth when you visited us in Edinburgh,

Mr Longreach. She will always be needed by her grandmamma and me.'

'I think, ma'am,' Daisy said crisply, 'you have stayed away too long and forget how many servants Toby employs. Elspeth must surely benefit from fresh air and a little exercise after the days spent in the coach.'

'I would enjoy a walk, Mama,' Elspeth said, thereby reminding them all that she had a voice and an opinion. 'I cannot think you and Grandmamma would deprive me of the chance against the possibility that your book or your knitting is in the wrong room.'

Reuben watched the contradictory feelings chase one another across Lady Beatrice's face. It was obvious that even she could think of no further argument that was not petty and might be construed as malicious. Her mama-in-law broke the tension.

'I think we might spare the girl for an hour, do not you, Beatrice? She will come home invigorated and more able to carry out her duties.'

'Certainly, Mrs Howie. If you believe the air in London is fresh enough to have that effect, Elspeth should be permitted to join her cousin,' Lady Beatrice conceded with ill grace and a shake of her head.

Reuben did not wait for further discussion, but was on his feet and crossing the floor to open the great doors onto the corridor. A footman waiting there stepped into the room and, following a quiet word from Daisy, crossed toward John Brent. Once at the guest's side, he offered a strong arm to ease Brent off the sofa and waited while he steadied himself. The shadow of Lucas Wellwood was a long one even in death, Reuben thought.

5

'I had decided Mrs Howie's influence was malign, but she swayed your mama's opinion over our walk,' John said to Elspeth as they made their way along Grosvenor Square. They managed four abreast, although once they left the wide pavements of the square, that would not be possible.

Daisy had to keep her steps in check because John was still moving very slowly. She glanced at Reuben under the brim of her bonnet and saw how easily he matched his tread to Elspeth's shorter one and, therefore, to John. She made a conscious effort to copy his plan.

'John, you have known my cousin for less than an hour and already you are criticising her grandmamma,' Daisy protested, but with little heat. She was beginning to think it would be a blessing to acquire a fever and perhaps some spots.

It would take her out of circulation for at least some of her relatives' visit.

'Don't fret, Lady Daisy, please. Mr Brent has struck gold with his observation. Grandmamma will be about some mischief while I am out of her orbit,' Elspeth spoke in matter-of-fact tones. 'In fact, I should not be surprised to return to the house and discover I have been removed to those attic bedrooms Mama remembers from her childhood.'

'Would you like to be removed, Elspeth? Not into the attics, of course, but there is a very pleasant room in my suite which I use for a study. There is a bed already installed.' Daisy caught her toe against the kerbstone as she spoke, and stumbled a little before Reuben caught her elbow. She shivered, as much at the memory of his words in the garden two nights ago as from the warmth of his strong fingers.

'Why, thank you,' Elspeth said with a cheerful laugh. 'Will you tell my mama the fire smokes or the drainpipe lets water into the corner of the wall?'

'Certainly I will, if that will help us

achieve our aim. I think Mrs Burtles may be applied to, and she will know what infelicity your mama might remember from childhood.' Daisy felt Reuben squeeze her arm before he let it go. Her behaviour over Elspeth was meeting with his approval. Would it continue to do so when he was irretrievably compromised? she wondered.

John interjected with enthusiasm, 'That's a good plan, my love. Housekeepers are a fund of information passed on to them by their predecessors and the other staff. Mrs Burtles will be able to think of a story to convince Lady Beatrice that the room is suitably inferior to others. Leave it to me, Miss Howie.'

Daisy cast a startled glance at her betrothed. John was always interested in domestic matters and staff intrigues, but he should be concentrating on getting better; on Toby; even on her, his new betrothed. Why was he directing his depleted energies toward Elspeth Howie?

'Thank you, Mr Brent,' Elspeth said with a laugh of joy. 'It is very pleasant to be walking out with young people.'

'Even when one of us reduces the pace to much as it would be with your grandmamma?' John asked.

'Why, no one minds in the circumstances, do we?' Elspeth's bright violet gaze captured Daisy's deeper brown one, and she was drawn to smile back. The girl was a great pleasure to be with, despite the trials of her existence.

'Of course we don't mind it, but perhaps you and Reuben would care to pick up your pace and John and I will catch up with you at the chapel,' Daisy suggested. 'There is an ever-present threat of thunder.'

'Is that why Stephens has sent a footman with umbrellas?' John asked, and they all laughed. Daisy looked round and saw the truth of his remark. Matt was walking at a respectful distance and carrying a bundle of umbrellas.

'We might take advantage of Daisy's suggestion, cousin Elspeth,' Reuben said, and offered her his arm. They were soon fifty or so yards ahead, and Daisy felt she had John's full attention for the first time since he had made his proposal.

'Do you and Mr Longreach know what goes forward with the Scottish family?' John asked, and Daisy briefly explained matters to him. 'My goodness, m'dear,' he said when she was done, 'I always knew Toby's life changed when Leo died, but this is beyond anything. Why did your mama not pursue this alliance when she was anxious to see Toby married?'

Daisy considered John's question. It was a puzzle because her mama had been keen to have Toby reinstated in society, and a respectable marriage would have been a very good beginning. Marriage to Elspeth would surely have been better than to Amarinta Wellwood.

'Perhaps she thought first cousins a bit too near for marriage,' she said tentatively. 'I would not say she does not have the highest regard for my aunt Beatrice, but they have never been close.'

'The woman is poisonous,' John said shortly. 'Must be a throwback, don't ye think?'

Daisy laughed. 'You have been known to call me a shrew.'

'My dear Daisy, anything I said in anger and pique when trying to make you understand the nature and depth of my feelings about our respective finances must now be disregarded, surely?' He smiled at her discomfiture. 'I find the Longreach clan on the whole to be a group of very likeable people.'

'Even Reuben?' Daisy asked in surprise.

'He is an interesting individual. I think his artistic temperament must persuade us to make allowances for some of the freaks of his conversation.' He offered her his arm, which she took. 'This side is good.'

'I am glad,' Daisy said, and she was. It was good to watch John's health restore itself.

As they neared the church porch, the opening notes of an organ voluntary reached them. Reuben was seizing opportunity again and playing a piece by Bach, whose work he adored.

Daisy turned John's words over in her

head. He was a stickler for correct form and behaviour. There was no prospect of him inviting her into the garden to walk in the moonlight, possibly even after they were married. Was that the cause of the deep breath she needed to calm her heartbeat when she thought about her distant cousin? It was a relief to know Reuben was living off the premises at present. She felt the reassuring solidity of John's arm. He would be everything she expected, and more.

The young people spent a pleasant half hour wandering around the interior of the magnificent Grosvenor Chapel while Reuben toyed with scraps of music. The sound swelled and died in the empty space before swelling again.

'I cannot think this organ will have been played to such advantage before,' John said.

'I played a concert here last week, in fact, Brent,' said Reuben. 'However, I do not think the audience was as appreciative as you all are.' He smiled and lowered his eyelids as Elspeth turned from her contemplation of some cross-stitched kneelers to watch his hands on the keys.

'Indeed,' she said. 'It is just like your visit to Edinburgh, Reuben, when we wandered among the churches and bribed the beadles to let you try out their pipe-organs, or play your violoncello to test the acoustics.'

'You went to Edinburgh to play organs?' Daisy asked.

She saw Reuben's shoulders tense, but he did not miss a note as he replied enigmatically, 'Perhaps, Daisy. Perhaps I wanted to know why Leo had tarried so long in the north.' He played a long climax of notes and smiled into Elspeth's eyes.

* * *

Daisy knew her mama and her aunt had crossed swords as soon as she caught sight of Stephens's pained expression when he opened the door for them on their return.

'Lady Daisy,' the butler said with a

long breath that avoided melodrama by a whisper. Daisy felt John's excitement mounting.

'Why Stephens, has something happened to upset you?' She cast a glance around but could see no evidence to indicate her aunt had authorised any furniture be moved or, as she had done once before on a passing visit, any walls to be painted.

'Upset me, your ladyship? Why, no, but Lady Mellon is up and going about. She is taking over the disposal of some of the rooms, and Mrs Burtles is threatening to resign her position,' the butler replied lugubriously.

John let out a satisfied half grunt, and Reuben began to walk a reluctant Elspeth toward the back corridor leading into the grounds. Daisy put out an arm. 'Thank you, Reuben, but I think Elspeth may be interested in the removals to which Stephens refers,' she said. Then she untied her bonnet and handed it to Smithers, who had arrived beside them.

'Well, then, Smithers,' John said with ill-concealed enthusiasm.

'Good day, sir. I am glad to say that Tilly is responding well to Mrs Burtles's care and will be able to attend Miss Fox in time for her visit to your sisters,' Smithers said calmly. Daisy knew the future countess's maid was not the cause of his excitement.

'I am very glad to have that news, Smithers.' He shuffled his weight from the good side to the bad and back again. 'Very glad. The visit is not planned until later in the week, however, and I think Lady Daisy was interested in whether her arrangements for everyone's comfortable disposition had been overset.'

'John,' Daisy remonstrated gently, but in truth she was holding onto her temper with difficulty. John should be taking their visitors up to the drawing-room and not interfering in the operation of the house. 'There is inclined to be a little needed by way of adjustment when a large party is settling in. Stephens, what is the issue most disturbing Mama?'

'And Mrs Burtles, Lady Daisy,' Stephens said. Daisy felt chill. Stephens so rarely allowed his personal feelings to colour his speech, and yet he wanted her to remember that his helpmeet was threatening resignation. 'Lady Beatrice and Mrs Howie continued to discuss the best distribution of the family after you and the other young people headed out. Mrs Howie ...'

Elspeth groaned at her side and Daisy turned to face her.

'I am so sorry, Lady Daisy. This is my fault.'

'In what way, Elspeth? Because you were born, perhaps? And do please stop calling me Lady Daisy. It makes me feel about thirty-five. Stephens?'

'Yes, m'lady. Mrs Howie volunteered to give up her room in the Indian suite should any senior member of Lady Mellon's family arrive from Spain. One thing led to another, and the ladies concluded it would be best if Miss Howie's belongings were moved forthwith to the green attics.'

‘I see,’ Daisy said. And she did. Her aunt knew full well that the green attics were reserved for the extra servants brought in when the house was full, as it would be over the days of the wedding. They were provoking a row, but Daisy could not understand why. Why did they continue to draw attention to Elspeth in these unfavourable ways? She might not be going to marry her cousin, the earl, but she was heir to her mama’s fortune, and would have no difficulty attracting a suitable husband. A tiny niggle of suspicion began in Daisy’s head.

‘Where is my mama, Stephens?’

‘In the drawing-room, m’lady. Lady Beatrice and Mrs Howie are in the garden, and Mrs Burtles is packing her trunk.’

‘We will go up,’ she said, and ushering Reuben with Elspeth ahead of her, waited while John gripped the banister rail and began his slow progress.

‘Perhaps you wish to go ahead, m’dear,’ John said hopefully. Daisy wondered if he really thought she didn’t see through his ruse.

'I will walk with you. Smithers, would you ask Mrs Burtles to attend in the drawing-room, please?'

Once the maid headed off toward the kitchens, John picked up his pace. Daisy allowed herself a small smile.

* * *

'Reuben, you honour us still with your presence,' Lady Mellon said as they entered the drawing-room. Elspeth hurried forward to kiss her aunt, and John made the best bow he was capable of in his present discomfort. Daisy nodded to Anna, her mama's companion, and crossed to the sofas arranged around the fireplace. No fire was burning, but the kindling was laid ready should the evening turn cool.

'I came to assist my cousin with her duties, but as you are restored to health, ma'am, perhaps I will take my leave,' said Reuben. 'I have to make several purchases in advance of my relatives' arrival.' He saw Elspeth comfortably seated before making his bows and departing.

'I do wonder over that young man,' Lady Mellon said with little emphasis. Daisy thought she probably was only vaguely aware of Reuben's presence or absence in the greater scheme of affairs going forward in the house at present.

'Daisy, your aunt has been spreading the usual chaos she brings with her, and now Mrs Burtles threatens to leave us. I am at a loss. The arrangements you made with the family are impeccable.'

'Why, thank you, Mama. I simply followed the plans I have watched you use in the past. Elspeth feels her grandmamma is the hand behind these manipulations.' Daisy smiled apologetically toward her cousin, but she need not have troubled about stepping on her sensibilities.

'Indeed, ma'am, I am so very sorry. It will be much easier for the entire party if I am moved into the attics.' Elspeth cast a pleading look toward her aunt, who gazed at her in open amazement.

'Elspeth, Frederick would come back

to haunt me if I sent his favourite niece to sleep in the attics on a thin mattress and iron bedstead. Please do not refer to the matter again. Daisy, I believe we should have Mrs Burtles in here to see if you can persuade her to give up this resignation,' Lady Mellon said.

'Why, Daisy has asked Smithers to send her up,' John said cheerfully. 'You do seem to get the hang of running a grand house with some ease, m'dear. Maybe I'll need to move.'

'Move?' Daisy breathed. 'Your family have been in Richmond for fifty years or more.'

'Yes, yes. We will see.'

Daisy was dismayed, but her thoughts were allowed no chance to dwell on this development because a sharp rap on the door brought Mrs Burtles into the room. A Mrs Burtles not hitherto encountered in Daisy's experience.

'There's no point in me being here to discuss things, your ladyships,' the housekeeper said with scarcely a curtsey and no more than a glance toward John and Elspeth. 'I will not be ordered around by no Mrs Howie whose son is no better than he should be, and that's saying nothing. Nothing at all.'

'Mrs Burtles,' Lady Mellon said with as much calm as if they were discussing the day's menus, Daisy thought, 'I am so grateful you were able to assist Daisy while I was laid low, but I am distressed that you intend to abandon me just as the earl is about to be married.' Her mama kept her eyes fixed on the housekeeper, and already that woman was taking deep breaths and fidgeting with her chatelaine of keys. Both ladies might have been alone in the room for all the attention they paid to anyone else.

'It's well and good for you to say so, Lady Mellon, your ladyship, but you have no conception of the heartache Lady Beatrice and her mama-in-law bring to this household,' Mrs Burtles said, determinedly refusing to look her employer in the eye. Daisy saw the way her fingers flicked the keys, making them rub against each other. 'Every time Lady Beatrice has visited, I have been subjected to lectures and harangues about how the late countess did things and how we have gone to extravagance and mismanagement in the kitchens since.'

'Indeed,' Lady Mellon said. Daisy noticed the tiny tic that appeared in her mama's cheek when she was being pushed towards anger. Surely Mama knew Aunt Beatrice thought that? Perhaps she did, but simply ignored it if it were not said in the drawing-room.

'I beg your pardon, my lady. I was a junior housemaid in the late countess's time as mistress here, and I am not able to agree with Lady Beatrice's remembrancing.'

'Nor I,' Lady Mellon said shortly. 'Mrs Burtles, I had hoped to persuade you to change your mind, but I can see it's made up. I will have my secretary write an impeccable reference for you and ask the earl's steward to make up your wages with three months extra to help you until you find another position.'

Daisy stared at her mama's set features

and then at Mrs Burtles's more mobile ones. She wondered if the woman was as perplexed as she herself felt. Surely her mama could not envisage the household running smoothly towards the wedding without Mrs Burtles? What was she thinking of?

6

'Daisy, I cannot apologise —'

Daisy clapped her hand over Elspeth's startled mouth and waited. When she was sure her cousin had subsided, she let her go.

The young people were arranged around some tables in the conservatory, having arrived there in a state of silent shock. This was little relieved by Stephens bringing trays of cold drinks. His accusing and desperate stare tugged at Daisy's heartstrings, and she could only shake her head in answer to his unspoken question. At her own waist, Mrs Burtles's chatelaine dangled in jingling accusation every time she moved. She was beginning to understand why Elspeth's instinct was to apologise for her existence, but she was not yet prepared to give up the struggle.

'The steward is sending out to the Registry in Regent Street, and Mama expects to interview several candidates this very afternoon,' she said eventually, but John only looked to her in bemusement, and Elspeth shook her head. 'Elspeth, may I ask whether my uncle and aunt have introduced you to any possible suitors since Leo's death?' Daisy felt uncomfortable as her cousin's beautiful eyes filled with pain. It was a very direct question, but she needed to find out why the Howies were behaving in such a curious manner. It lacked all semblance of gentility.

'Yes, of course. Grandmamma believes a young woman should be married by the age of twenty, and I am past that by some years,' Elspeth said in more agitation than she had shown. 'I have been forced to refuse three offers from a gentleman of advanced years who was in the Edinburgh High School with my papa.'

'Gawd!' John exclaimed, and Daisy glanced his way. He was flushed, and the bruising on his face stood out in ever deepening yellows and purples.

'The same gentleman?' Daisy asked.

'Three offers from the same gentleman?'

'He has recently suffered financial setbacks, and I think my papa wishes to secure his future through my inheritance,' Elspeth said. Her agitation was growing. 'Do you think I should have accepted my parents' guidance in this matter?'

'No!' John said with no less vehemence than his previous utterance. 'Gawd! One hears tell of parents who imprison their daughters and feed them on bread and water until they agree to unsuitable matches. It sounds to me as if Lady Beatrice and Mr Howie are of that mould.'

'If he is as old as your papa, Elspeth, surely he won't live long enough to benefit from your inheritance, as you don't receive it until your mama dies?'

'That's correct. You have yours directly from our great grandmamma because you are the next female in your line, but I must wait while my mama lives. My mama is in good health.' Elspeth drew a deep breath, and Daisy watched the girl's small hands open and close where they lay on the table. 'But Mr Beatson has several daughters and nothing to bestow on them. I think it is envisaged the trustees would release money to me on my marriage and that could in turn be used to fund dowries for the girls.'

'It is very strange, is it not, that Mr Howie prefers to think of the interest of others' children before his own?' John said.

'He didn't think this way until I refused to make any effort to secure Tobias's interest. A canker seemed to enter his head then, and he began to listen to Grandmamma's complaints.' Elspeth drew a small handkerchief from her reticule and dabbed her eyes. 'She is so very anxious for me to have a title, and cannot understand my disinterest.'

'And yet she has no title of her own besides mistress,' Daisy mused aloud. 'It is entirely respectable to be the wife of a gentleman.'

'Of course,' Elspeth agreed. She tucked the linen away and squared her shoulders. 'However, my grandmamma is elderly, and her opinions, once formed, are difficult to overturn.'

'Hmm,' John murmured and Daisy cast an enquiring glance his way. 'I have heard talk like this in my club, y'know. There is a snobbery about lineage that some take to extremes. Lucas Wellwood, for example. He not only wanted the Mellon wealth by association, but also he wanted titled matches for himself and his sister.'

'We know where that led,' Daisy said, closing the subject decisively. She stood up and waved John back when he would have risen. 'Don't struggle to rise, please. I must go and attend to more of the housekeeper's duties. I will join you both again shortly.'

'As to that, my love, surely you would appreciate my assistance with these domestic matters? I believe I can explain things to Stephens, man to man.'

Daisy saw the naked longing in her betrothed's eyes. He wanted to glean as much of the downstairs gossip as he could and did not relish being kept out of it. She weighed the issues in her head. On the one hand, John was well-liked by the staff and could ease the tensions that had built up in the house. On the other, Daisy needed to find out why her mama had let Mrs Burtles go without a fight. She strongly suspected there was a plan afoot to which she was not yet a party, and there was little hope of prising that out of her mama while John made garrulous and overpowering suggestions in the background.

'Thank you, but I will deal with this,' she said. 'You said earlier you have been sleeping in the afternoons, John. Do you wish to retire?'

'Who would look after Miss Howie, were I to do that?'

'Please, Mr Brent, you must recover your strength before the wedding,' Elspeth interceded before Daisy could point out that John had been intending to abandon her when the prospect of gossip was ripe. 'I will go up to the new room I am to occupy in Daisy's suite and attend to some sewing while the light is good.'

Daisy cast her older cousin a grateful smile. There was enough unhappiness in the household without her quarrelling with John. She wondered briefly about the sewing Elspeth referred to. If it was, as she suspected, an attempt to 'make over' some of the woeful dresses she had already worn, then Daisy needed to hatch a plan of her own with Smithers.

* * *

'Daisy!'

She was ascending from the basement when she heard Lady Beatrice call from a step halfway up the grand staircase. She unashamedly decided she must be afflicted by sudden, if selective, deafness, and ducked into a recessed doorway.

'Mrs Howie, was that not Lady Daisy crossing the landing?' She heard her aunt's aggrieved complaint to her mama-in-law with little compassion. She had done her fill of duty towards her aunt for one day.

The door she was pressed against led into a minor reception room, and she gasped in surprise as it fell open behind her. She would have landed in an ignominious heap, had strong arms not reached for her and broken her fall.

'Steady there,' spoke a deep voice, threatening laughter. 'We all wish to avoid our relatives at some time or other, but there wouldn't be much gained if you broke a leg in the flight.'

'Reuben.' Daisy was as much relieved to be saved from a bump as she was surprised to find him behind the door. 'You were skulking.'

'I was.'

'Because?' Daisy turned to face him now that she had regained her balance. She fixed her open gaze on his more quizzical one. If Reuben thought to gammon her with any nonsense, she would see it there in his expression.

'You have not changed very much since we boys held you upside down over the carp pond out at m'father's estate,' Reuben said. 'Still charging into everything with no thought for what the consequences might bring you to.'

'Do not remind me of those carp. I smelled of fish and pondweed for two weeks after,' she said, but a smile tugged at her mouth. 'I might have drowned.'

'An outside possibility, but even the minor soaking need not have happened if you hadn't wriggled so much.'

'No? However, it did result in Mama dismissing all the nursery staff without characters.'

'A most unfortunate outcome.'

'Why so? I hated Nanny Cavey. She would go on and on over nothing at all.' Daisy saw that her words had made Reuben thoughtful.

'M'father took all of us boys, including Toby, who had really nothing to do with it, into the stables and beat us with his walking cane. He said we had to learn to think of others, and that those four women would not easily get new posts without characters from your mama's steward.' Reuben tried for a laugh, but Daisy saw only a ghost of a smile on his mobile features.

'Oh. Did they get other posts?'

'I was a child at the time, Daisy. There was no way I could find out.' Reuben hesitated before going on. 'Tobias gave m'father his quarter's allowance to pass on to them so they would not starve while they searched. Two of the younger girls had come from the Foundling Home and did not have relatives to breach the interval.'

'Goodness! And all because I was bored to distraction being ladylike in the nursery attics.' She moved across the room and looked out onto the large square, hoping to allow Reuben a moment to recover his composure, but also partly to think about how selfish a six-year-old could be. Surely she had learned to be more thoughtful of her servants? Smithers, who'd spent several years in the Foundling Hospital, now regarded the household in Grosvenor Square as her family. How awful it would be to be turned off without a character.

'Don't repine on it, Daisy. We are all older and more aware of our duty.'

'Even if I am unchanged?' She turned back into the room and sent a challenging look towards the man.

'You throw my words back at me when I was caught by surprise and spoke without much thought. First you stand on my toes in the drawing-room …'

'You were out of order, sir, kissing my hand.'

'And gazing into your deep brown eyes so very like my own.'

'Reuben!'

'Daisy. May a man not tell his cousin how she reminds him of all that is good about his family?' As he set his head to one side, Daisy heard the strident tones of her aunt berating a footman. 'When certain other members of the family are most intent on bringing it into disrepute?'

She suppressed the impulse to run but raised an eyebrow in enquiry. How were they to avoid meeting Lady Beatrice on the staircase? she wondered, and Reuben sensed it. He pointed towards the door connecting the room they stood in with another, set on a corner of the house, which would let them escape onto its secondary staircase. She nodded silently and slipped across the carpet. Reuben turned the brass handle and pushed the door open. Daisy passed into the gap between the rooms and waited while he closed the first door behind them, before stretching her hand to the handle of the one leading into the next. It was dark, and the handle was not at the height she expected. Reuben's arm came around her, and she felt the flex of his muscles against her chest. She stumbled.

'Carefully, little cousin,' Reuben murmured in her ear. 'If we attract your aunt's attention to us, Brent will find himself in want of a fiancée.' His arm closed around her and held her upright.

Daisy's clothing constricted her breathing. The warmth of Reuben's breath on her nape was like a caress. His words were a whisper of sound loosed into the darkness. Individual hairs stood away from her skin as goose-bumps lifted along her arms. Was it simply his breath, or was she feeling the touch of warm lips?

He smelled of tobacco and sandalwood; damp wool and coffee. Emotion flooded her veins with overpowering heat, and she slumped against him.

'Oh, my dear girl, not now.' The words were a sharp reminder to Daisy. This was not a game of hunt the robber, when they would be discovered by other cousins and joined in their dark hiding place until the door could not be drawn closed and the giggles no longer be suppressed. This was her brother's house, and her unattached, very male cousin pressed against the sheer silk of her morning gown. This was the threat of ruin to her reputation and heartbreak for her fiancé. It was madness beyond anything.

Reuben released her waist and opened the door into startling sunshine. As they half-fell, half-stumbled into the corner room, Toby turned from contemplation of the garden and raised both eyebrows in astonishment.

'Well, well, Reuben. Still here?' the earl said, and Daisy knew her colour fluxed from carmine to white and back in the passing of seconds. How would they explain this?

'As you see, Toby. Daisy needed rescuing ...'

'Again? You make a habit of finding young ladies in need of rescuing, do you not?'

Daisy gazed in astonishment at her brother's hard features. His odd choice of words flummoxed her. Why wasn't he asking Reuben different questions? Why didn't he fly into the boughs and create a scene?

'Miss Howie does well against the slingshots used by her relatives, but I formed the impression Daisy needed back-up over her aunt's strictures.' Reuben stepped to one side as he spoke, and straightened the cuffs of his linen shirt where they peeped from his coat sleeves. 'That's why I did not take myself off as I had told Lady Mellon I would, but occupied an hour in practising the piece I will play at my next recital.'

'I see,' Toby replied. Daisy gripped the back of a nearby chair. She gazed at her brother, who made no comment on their arrival in an apparently deserted chamber from a hallway no wider than the depth of the walls. 'Yes, I see. Daisy, I did want to find you, as I think you might give the chatelaine back to the housekeeper now. I do value your assistance in looking after our relatives, but I cannot have you employed as a domestic.'

Daisy gaped.

'Don't, my dear,' Toby said with maddening condescension. 'You look a little like one of the carp from my late uncle's pond.'

'Do I? And why do I feel as if you men have been reminiscing?' Daisy asked as calmly as she could manage. Irritation over the men's casual exchange overcame her fear of Toby's anger. They were in collusion. She was abruptly more confident of it than of anything. 'Tell me, Toby, why are you sure Mama and Mrs Burtles will settle their grievances?'

'Because I have told both of them that I will not countenance any change in my arrangements before Miss Fox takes over the reins of the household. Mrs Burtles is back in harness, and Mama is fuming in the library.' Toby crossed to the door onto the corridor and would have opened it, but Daisy's next words stayed his hand.

'So Mama's distress and my inconvenience, Miss Howie's embarrassment and Mrs Burtles's fury, are as nothing when Miss Fox might be incommoded.'

'Do not forget yourself, Daisy. Miss Fox will be my countess in a few days' time. Should you and Mama wish to go and live in the Dower House at that moment, then please do so, but do not think you can leave behind chaos for the new mistress.' Toby's eyes now snapped with anger. It was only a little less intense than that which Daisy felt.

'I am in no way accountable for the behaviour of our aunt, Toby. You do me a grave injustice, and threaten to drive a wedge between the new countess and her relatives that was not there before,' she said, proud of the steady timbre of her voice. Only last month, she might have felt the threatening heat of tears. Today she was pushed beyond her endurance, but she was not babyish.

'Cousins,' Reuben said, drawing both pairs of chocolate-brown eyes to his bemused expression. 'Cousins, we forget that the underlying cause of this unhappiness is Lady Beatrice and her Edinburgh preoccupations.'

Daisy blinked. What an odd expression. What, she wondered, did Reuben mean by that? Toby moved back into the room from the door. Why did it bring her brother instantly to heel?

'You're right, man. Daisy, my dear, forgive me. Please take the keys back to Stephens or Mrs Burtles, and if you can, find a way to entertain Miss Howie.'

'Miss Howie was talking about altering a dress of her mama's for the wedding ceremony, Toby,' Reuben interrupted. 'This morning while we walked ahead of Daisy and Brent, she told me of several dresses she has brought with her that will be so very suitable if she finds enough time to alter them before the celebrations begin in earnest.' Reuben studied his fingers, and Daisy let her glance slide from one man to the other. Toby's complexion fired as the silence extended among them. She shook out her skirts.

'She was wearing the most woeful travelling costume of washed-out tweed when she arrived,' she said. 'And her gowns since then have been more serviceable than fashionable, or even pretty.' She yanked the chatelaine, expecting it to come away, but the cord tangled and the keys hung limply as low as her knees.

'Daisy, stop fighting with that thing. You're giving me a headache,' Toby snapped.

'It's caught. I can't free it,' she protested, and then wished she'd kept trying because Reuben stepped forward and lifted the heavy bunch of keys. He draped them over his arm and glanced briefly into her flushed face before dropping his gaze to the knot she'd made. He worked away at it with exaggerated patience. It slipped out, and Reuben grabbed the bundle before it clanged to the floor.

'We don't want Aunt Beatrice in here,' he said shortly.

'No, we don't,' Toby agreed. 'Elspeth's

dresses are serviceable?'

'They were. Unfortunately, I believe they will by now have had an accident rendering them unusable,' Daisy said while studying the golden flecks in Toby's eyes. Would he understand the nuances of her little speech?

He appeared to make up his mind. 'Daisy, would you please take our cousin shopping? The carriage is at your disposal with James and one of the footmen.'

'What if Miss Howie has not been given an allowance?' Daisy asked. There was little left of her own allowance, but she would happily make it available to her cousin. 'I think her mama keeps tight purse strings.'

'Undoubtedly in that respect, my aunt does keep her money close. Ask the modiste and the merchants to send the bills to my steward, only do make sure our cousin is fittingly dressed to enjoy her stay.'

'Toby?'

'You're not deaf, Daisy. How much permission does a female need to go shopping at her brother's expense?'

* * *

Reuben watched the door close fully behind Daisy before he turned to his cousin, the earl. As he'd feared, Toby was only waiting for privacy.

'It's all very well for me to say you must do what needs to be done, but I fear that licence does not include being found in passageways the size of a small linen closet with my sister.'

'No, sir. The circumstances were exceptional,' Reuben offered.

'Where Daisy is concerned, it would be a minor miracle if any circumstances were not. We are at a stand, man,' Toby said. 'You realise the fuss Lady Beatrice would have made if she had been the one waiting here?'

'I knew Lady Beatrice was still on the stairs, and I could hear doors being opened and closed along the landing above. No doubt she sent a footman ahead.' Reuben paced. Toby was expecting a great deal of him, but both men knew how high the stakes were.

'Yes.' Toby took in a deep gulp of air. 'I am overwrought. Gawd, I never thought to hear those words issue from my own lips, but so it is. Until Mrs Barlow presented herself at the courts with Rodney Perkins, the outcome looked bleak.' Reuben studied the lines of strain marking his cousin's handsome features as he made this confession.

'You are a belted earl. Surely their lordships could not find fault with your evidence?' Reuben asked, although he suspected many would find fault *because* Toby was a peer. 'Besides, you are about to enter the marriage of your desire.'

'Am I?' Toby ran his hands through his hair and down across the stubble around his chin. 'Do you not realise how skittish Miss Fox is over all this? If she can find any way out of fulfilling her promise by pretending it would suit me better to be relieved of my betrothal, she will.'

'Toby, she needs your reassurance. Go to her.'

'How can I go to her when her maid is only this morning able to stand unaided and my aunt is causing mayhem? I had no business shouting at Daisy, but what I was shouting about is very true. Lady Beatrice wants to bring chaos to the household and by so doing make Miss Fox back off.'

'It can be daunting for a young female without experience to take over an establishment such as this.' Reuben shrugged. 'Lady Mellon will not abandon her while she learns the ins and outs.'

'No, Mama would not do that. Only, if she had quarrelled with me — if a quarrel had been engineered between us — she and Daisy might be miles away in the Dower House in Hampshire. What then?' Toby sounded less sure of himself than he ever had, and Reuben gathered his thoughts.

'We will defeat Lady Beatrice, sir. We have a lot of advantage on our side, as she is unaware of the extent of our knowledge about her . . . ' He hesitated. It still took a little courage to refer to Lady Beatrice as a criminal, and he drew breath. ' . . . misappropriations.' He saw Toby's chin come up and was glad he'd found the right way to tackle his cousin's black mood. He only hoped it would deflect the earl's memory of seeing Daisy come out of the door.

'You are right,' Toby said in clipped tones, 'and I am to take Miss Fox to stay with John at Richmond. His sisters wish to make her closer acquaintance. I must make her understand I want her to be my countess, despite everything that has taken place.'

'Were our relationship still the more equal one we enjoyed when Leo lived, I might have offered a suggestion in relation to Miss Fox and country isolation.' Reuben watched his cousin and boyhood friend, now the earl and head of their family, pace over priceless carpets. He let his mind drift to their first encounters with the fair sex. Any thoughts of earldoms were at a comfortable distance in those heady days, and the youths revelled in health, good looks, and ready cash. At that time, he would not have had to cloak his meaning in suggestion, but would have said outright …

'You are suggesting I should anticipate my vows?'

'Whatever plans Lady Beatrice has afoot, Miss Fox will be unlikely to walk away if she has enjoyed the marriage bed, albeit in advance of the ceremony.'

He felt Toby's gaze pierce him with rapier-like intensity. What would his cousin think of that suggestion? Would Reuben be requested never to darken the doors of Grosvenor Square again?

'There will be no report of the success or failure of any such operation, Reuben. It is a clever suggestion, however. There could be no possibility of annulment.'

Reuben bowed. His mind was in turmoil. Where had he found the gall to suggest his cousin should visit such immoral behaviour on his innocent bride? Times were odd.

He walked ahead of Toby and opened the door onto the corridor. Lady Beatrice, large and red, stood with her hand raised towards the handle. One of the junior footmen waited impassively, three or four steps behind her.

'Ma'am,' Reuben said. 'Have you lost your way?'

'Mr Longreach and Tobias.' Lady Beatrice's features fell in almost comical confusion.

'Good morning, Aunt. May I assist you with anything?' Toby spoke as if this was the only object of his existence, and Reuben was impressed by his sang-froid.

'No, sir. I was seeking my niece, but you gentlemen are unaccompanied. How strange. I did believe I saw Daisy enter a door around the corner, and yet that room is also empty.' Lady Beatrice sent a quick glance over the room, searching for unaccounted nieces. Reuben prayed he'd closed the connecting door fully so that it would not attract her attention, and forced himself not to turn toward it.

'Daisy is preparing for a shopping expedition, Aunt, and will be asking Elspeth to attend her. If I can do nothing more for you, I must closet myself with my steward. He has many matters of business requiring my attention.'

'Of course, Tobias. I know that your position as earl is not the sinecure some think it.'

'And I must go to my lodgings, where I hope to find my own family safely arrived. Toby, Lady Beatrice.' Reuben bowed to both and strode off.

7

Daisy settled into the Mellon town coach and smiled at her companions. Elspeth was drinking in the sights as they made slow progress through heavy traffic. Smithers was wearing a closed expression that Daisy knew would cost her a golden guinea at the very least.

'It takes no more than twenty minutes to reach Mademoiselle Juliette's salon, Elspeth. Fortunately, I had an appointment already in her book,' Daisy lied, hoping fervently that Perkins had been able to impress upon Mademoiselle the importance of seeing them immediately.

'Yes, that is fortunate,' Elspeth agreed. 'I do think some of the dresses might have been rescued. Are you absolutely sure it was bleach you dropped them into, Smithers?'

'Yes, miss, bleach. I'm ever so sorry, miss. I can't think how, as it hasn't happened before. Normally I'm so very careful — but then, the house is busier than usual.'

Daisy watched Smithers lower her gaze from Elspeth's anxious expression and study her cotton gloves. The maid didn't seem to be having any problem with the scenario Daisy had presented to her, and so far, Elspeth was taken in.

'I am overwhelmed by Tobias's offer to replace them.'

'The earl is always an understanding master, miss. He wouldn't want to dock my wages over a genuine accident,' Smithers said.

'No,' Elspeth agreed, even more doubtfully. 'My mama, however, would have no such conscience.'

'I am sure Aunt Beatrice will have little to complain of when she learns all the gowns have been replaced by new ones at Toby's expense.' Daisy felt the carriage jolt and was pleased to see they were outside Mademoiselle Juliette's. She risked a glance along the pavement and saw Perkins waiting under the striped awning of the salon. He looked towards the carriage and lifted a hand in salute to James, the coachman, and his companion Conor who had asked to be included in the drive. Apparently the chance to experience London traffic was one an Edinburgh coachman did not wish to miss out on. Daisy took a deep breath. It was the signal she'd agreed with Perkins. Mademoiselle Juliette would see them and pretend there was an appointment in place. Perkins strode off towards Grosvenor Square and the ladies began to climb down.

'Is that not one of your house servants, Daisy? Perkins, is it?' Elspeth asked as she poked her head out of the carriage door and waited while Daisy stepped onto the pavement. 'He is walking at a smart pace.'

'Perkins?' Daisy repeated feebly. Drat! She had no idea Elspeth had even encountered Toby's man.

'I don't think it can have been Mr Perkins,' Smithers said helpfully. 'But I have heard him talk of his brother, Rodney, who works for a family in

Albemarle Street. I expect they look alike, miss.'

'That's probably the answer, Smithers,' Daisy said gratefully. 'Tell me, did the earl say anything about a present to you to mark his betrothal? I wondered whether you still hankered after one of Mademoiselle Juliette's exquisite parasols?' Daisy swung her own parasol and smiled at her maid. It would take all of the remainder of her quarter's allowance, but there was no doubt Smithers had earned it.

'Why no, Lady Daisy. There is to be a celebration in the servants' hall, of course.'

'Of course, but I do think a parasol would be just the thing to set off your grey stripe. There was a deep rose shade available the last time I visited.' Daisy led the small party into the salon, and the coachmen, with Matt the footman, settled to a long wait.

* * *

Daisy sighed. Mademoiselle had risen ably to the challenge of dressing Elspeth, and they were now in possession of two morning gowns and an evening gown for regular use to carry home, together with a substantial collection of silk stockings, under-linen, nightwear, shawls, and a coat suitable for the theatre. Several more formal gowns were on order and would be delivered at the earliest opportunity with matching cloaks and gloves.

'*Un moment*,' Mademoiselle said. 'I 'ave a most perfect ensemble for the young lady to wear to the evening ball.' She left the main salon in a flourish of skirts and trailing tapes, and was back in an instant carrying an exquisite gown of larkspur blue.

The three younger women let out a collective breath and all spoke at once.

'Oh, miss, that's the perfect match for your eyes,' Smithers said.

'Elspeth, it is irresistible,' Daisy said. She reached a hand toward the flowing silks and their net overlay. Elspeth would be ethereal in such a gown.

'Mama would never permit me to wear such a beautiful dress,' Elspeth said in the matter-of-fact tone Daisy was beginning to dread.

'Then we must take great care she does not see it in advance,' Daisy spoke with decision. The plan to marry her cousin off had begun to form in her head as her aunt had pounded around the corridors earlier. Why should the woman wield such power as to consign her beautiful cousin to the role of ugly duckling forever? Daisy thought it was monstrous. She swallowed a lump in her throat. Reuben was in need of a wife to arrange his affairs and bring powerful benefactors to his concerts. Elspeth was not much known in London at present, but as the cousin of the Earl of Mellon and a well-dressed beauty, such as Daisy could present her, then she soon would be.

'Daisy?' Elspeth's voice held the hint of a question, and she realised she'd been allowing her attention to wander. 'Is this not the colour Mr Brent described as his favourite? Should you not try this gown on?'

'John does like the flower. His sisters

grow it in drifts in their gardens at Richmond, but I think you must wear it.' Daisy sat down on one of the chairs Mademoiselle provided and waved Elspeth toward the curtain concealing a small changing area. Smithers went with her, and in a matter of two or three minutes the reluctant debutante was robed in layers of silk and net that whispered and sighed as she moved.

'Come into the front shop,' the modiste urged. 'There we 'ave the larger mirrors.'

They moved through, and Daisy saw other people were waiting for Mademoiselle's personal attention. There was a rustle of interest as Elspeth walked shyly across the deep pile of the salon's carpets. Her cousin had transformed from a dowdy country visitor into an elegant woman whose town bronze would be the envy of many. Daisy choked a little before she caught hold of her sentiments. This was no moment for careless tears.

'Why, Miss Howie,' Reuben said as he rose from a banquette.

Daisy started. What was he doing in a

fashionable modiste's salon? Surely he didn't keep a mistress? The question was monstrous, but what did she really know of Reuben's life beyond the cloistered atmosphere of home?

'Mr Longreach,' Elspeth said in some confusion.

'Reuben. You are everywhere,' Daisy spoke tartly. A second person, a lady, rose as they approached. 'And you bring another cousin. Charlotte, how lovely.' She embraced the young woman with Reuben. 'Elspeth, this is Reuben's sister, Charlotte.' Daisy made the introduction and knew her voice was coloured by relief. Reuben had brought his sister to visit the salon. That was a perfectly respectable expedition. He was not here ordering gowns for a mistress. She had no business allowing her imagination to run away with her common sense.

'Good day, cousin Daisy,' Charlotte said. She was a young woman in her early twenties, and although much liked by Daisy, not often seen in town. Charlotte was betrothed to a major whose regiment was currently abroad. She expected to be married in the autumn, and the family knew she would then retire with her husband to his small country estate and grow babies and barley.

'Miss Longreach.' Elspeth dropped a polite curtsey. 'It is very exciting to meet so many of the family I have only read of in Mama's correspondence before now.'

'Charlotte, please. Yes, I am looking forward to Tobias's marriage festivities, and Reuben has persuaded me to spend some of my pin money on a gown for the pre-wedding ball.' Charlotte smiled at the group. 'When I see the quality and the effect of Mademoiselle's handiwork, I am so very glad to have agreed.'

Reuben had *persuaded her to come.* Daisy stored the information in her head to think about later. What were her brother and her cousin about? Were they the same things?

'Elspeth Howie, you look beautiful in that colour, which is an almost exact match for your eyes,' Reuben said.

Elspeth blushed. 'Do you think I might wear it?'

'Forgive me; I have made you blush. Of course you might wear it. Have you not already told her so, Daisy?'

'I have,' Daisy said firmly. 'Now, cousins, if you will excuse us, we have to visit several other warehouses and be back in time to dress for dinner.'

'Other warehouses?' Elspeth said in fading accents. Daisy quelled a sigh. Where was the bright and confident young woman she remembered?

'Yes, others. Shoes and a riding habit, for example, are not bought from Mademoiselle.'

'I cannot need a riding habit, Daisy. I do not ride,' Elspeth protested.

'Then it will be shoes only, but they need careful study and can be time-consuming to purchase,' Daisy said. 'Charlotte, will you not accompany us?'

'I would be honoured to assist, and indeed, need to buy some kid slippers to complete my own outfit. Mademoiselle's assistant has taken my measurements, and I am to return here tomorrow when some gowns will be ready for my inspection.'

Daisy saw the satisfied expression fly across Reuben's features before he schooled it to polite civility. He had engineered this meeting, she thought with a clarity that robbed her of breath. He wanted her to invite Charlotte into this little circle.

* * *

The gentlemen came noisily into the drawing-room later that evening, and Daisy glanced away from the tea tray to their untidy procession. It was difficult to remember that all of these men had seen military or naval service at some time. With the exception of Toby and Reuben, they were portly and lame to varying degrees — even John, but of course he was still recovering from cracked ribs. It was not fair to criticise him.

One by one she filled their orders for

tea until only Reuben waited. He was conversing quietly with an uncle from the Newcastle area about this year's summer calving. Daisy yawned. Instantly she lowered her head to conceal it. How long would it be before she could seek the peace of her own room?

'You are tired, my dear,' Reuben said, and she sent him a small smile. 'Such a pity I am incarcerated in lodgings. I might have played some soothing piece to lull you to sleep.'

'I have enjoyed listening to your practice pieces,' she said.

'A reluctant admission. But like all performers, I accept any praise with gratitude.' Reuben made a tiny bow. 'Brent seems much taken with Charlotte and Elspeth Howie. He spends so many hours with females, I would have expected him to relish male company more than he appears to do.' He stirred the tea in his dish with a tiny spoon.

Not for the first time, Daisy's eyes were drawn to the supple strength of his fingers. She remembered their warmth as they had circled around her hand in the dark. A hot flush stole up her neck until she reached for the fan by her side and snapped it open. Drat this man. No one else caused her to lose her composure to such an extent. She saw the tiny movement of his eyebrow that told her he had seen her discomfort.

'John is good company for both sexes, and he has relieved Toby of much of the duty of entertaining our relatives.' She shut her fan and stood up. Reuben stepped to one side to let her ease out from behind the tea-table.

'And what about you, my dear? Will your mama be fully restored to her position soon enough to let you enjoy John's company before he goes back to Richmond with Toby and Miss Fox?'

'Truth to tell, I keep forgetting Toby and John have made this arrangement. The Brent ladies will have many years to get to know Mariah. I cannot quite see its urgency.' She heard John's laughter and glanced round in time to see him pat Elspeth gently on her arm.

The older girl positively sparkled tonight. Smithers had dressed her hair, and Daisy had loaned her a Spanish silk shawl inherited from a visiting relative. It combined with the flashing golds and ambers of her new gown to enhance her looks beyond anything one might have thought possible. Across the room, Aunt Beatrice scowled, and Mrs Howie sat in silent outrage.

'No need to worry about John's interest there, my dear. Charlotte will be able to take her around and leave you in peace with your fiancé.' Reuben bowed and took his remaining tea across the room to speak to Aunt Mathilde.

Daisy stared at his retreating back. What could he possibly mean? She glanced again at John and sighed. He was making such an effort to make the guests welcome. Who would not love him?

8

'Daisy, my love, did I tell you how I resolved the argument between my man and Amelia's maid?' John asked on the following morning when Daisy and he were unaccompanied.

'I believe you did.' Daisy set her bonnet on the seat beside her. The sun was struggling to pierce a heavy cloud cover and would not trouble her complexion, she was sure. She shook free the weight of her chestnut curls in the hope John might notice how thick and lustrous they were since Smithers had treated them with a rinsing agent made from a new French recipe. 'It was very thoughtful of you to hide the sweetmeats until only Draker was in the room.'

'Yes, and Elspeth Howie agreed it was the only thing to do. Why, she is the most astute female, apart from yourself, my love. She has much to do in keeping hold of the servants in her parents' Edinburgh house; Mrs Howie is difficult, if not cantankerous, to work for.' John sat down carefully, but Daisy saw he was more supple than yesterday.

'You are more able to sit and stand than even yesterday. I think Stephens can have his footman back.' Daisy spoke to the servant assigned to them by Stephens and watched him retreat into the house. There was enough heavy work to do without one of the men having to be on hand to ease John off the garden furniture.

'Daisy, are you sure Mrs Burtles has decided to remain?' John asked, and she struggled to conceal a sigh. 'I ask only because Tilly returns with me to Richmond tomorrow in advance of Mariah's visit.'

'You think Mrs Burtles stayed on in order to help Tilly recover fully from her injuries?' Daisy asked, but she conjured the memory of Toby's snapping anger. Her brother clearly believed he was in charge of his staff, and had sorted the problem to Mrs Burtles's satisfaction. 'I think Toby believes otherwise.'

'Toby. What does Toby know about human nature?'

'Quite a lot, I believe. He was thought to be a good leader when in the army.'

'That was of men, my love. The questions here are to do with the peculiar jealousies arising among women. On that subject, I am much better qualified than most to opine.' John took a deep breath, but he had forgotten the extent of his injuries and, instead of adding girth to his frame, he crumpled in pain.

Daisy frowned. 'John, do we have to discuss my brother's staff? There has been so little time for us to get to know one another since our betrothal that I feel we should not waste this precious opportunity.' She smiled even more winningly, but John struggled to breathe, and when he recovered, seemed determined to have the last word on this issue.

'I am sorry to return to the subject. I know Toby believes Mrs Burtles to be satisfied, as Stephens told me so this morning.'

'You have been discussing the household with Stephens?' Daisy tried to keep censure from her voice but saw the flash of irritation cross John's brow.

'I had to consult Stephens, as you and Toby have kept the matter very close. Even Reuben Longreach knows more than I did.' John tapped a tattoo on his thigh with one hand. 'When we are setting up our own household, I expect to be consulted on such matters. A gentleman needs to know his staff are happy. Happy staff create a happy household.'

'My papa was not much interested in the running of the household, and I suppose from him I assume gentlemen simply take an interest when things go wrong, and their comfort might be disturbed — as Toby did yesterday.' Daisy smoothed the silk of her new morning gown. John had yet to tell her how becoming the emerald inserts on the bodice were, and she had given him ample opportunity to notice.

'Exactly. *When things have gone wrong*. Toby would have done much better to concern himself along the way and prevented things from going wrong,' John said, with a touch of triumph Daisy found she did not care for.

'You mistake matters, John, if you think any of us can predict what my aunt will do to upset the staff in advance of her doing it.'

'Now there you are wrong. Stephens says Reuben had warned him to be on the look-see where your aunt is concerned.' John stood slowly up from the garden bench. 'The lady is approaching. Perhaps we should continue this discussion later.'

Daisy lifted her head in confusion. What on earth was Stephens talking about, and why was he sharing such information with John? Her aunt was coming along the path, however, and there was no time to do anything other than throw John an enquiring glance. He grinned back at her with the exuberance of a small boy.

'Aunt Beatrice,' Daisy said as her aunt came up to them. 'Good morning.'

'Daisy,' her aunt wheezed. 'I have been seeking your attention for an unconscionable time. Where did you disappear to yesterday afternoon?'

'I went shopping with Elspeth, ma'am. She wore one of our purchases at dinner.' The malicious gleam in her aunt's eye should have warned Daisy, and it did, but too late for her to take avoiding action.

'Don't play smart games with me, my lady. I sought your assistance on the main staircase and you chose to ignore me. When I tried to find you, I came across the earl and Reuben Longreach. Both looking as guilty as anything I have had the misfortune to encounter anywhere.'

'I am unable to answer you, ma'am. The earl surely does not require permission to be in any part of his own house, and if Reuben was in his company, then how does he trespass?' Daisy kept hold of her temper with difficulty. Reuben had behaviour to be guilty over, but the idea he would give it away by wearing guilt on his face was too simple. What had Toby to be guilty over? She suspected her aunt was spearing for information.

'How does he trespass? Why, Mr

Brent should know this — he trespasses by playing games of hide-me find-me with young women in tight passageways.' Lady Beatrice spat the words at them and Daisy took a step back. The woman was deranged with frustration.

'I say, Lady Beatrice, you'll work your sensibilities into a nervous fit if you allow a minor incident to assume such proportions,' John said, and Daisy remembered why she loved him. He never mistrusted her.

'How dare you address me thus,' Lady Beatrice said darkly.

'It's for your own good, ma'am,' John said. 'Sit here, and I'll find Mrs Howie to come to you.' He strode off towards the house, and Daisy watched as her aunt sank onto the bench.

'Don't think I don't know you were skulking in that connecting passageway with Reuben, Daisy Mellon. I will make this buffoon you're betrothed to understand how it is between you two, no matter how slow his understanding.'

Daisy recoiled. What was the canker

in her aunt's brain? 'Aunt Beatrice, I think John is right. You are becoming overwrought.'

'You think to fob me off, girl. I have seen the looks you exchange with that man. You would deserve each other if circumstances were different. He with his need for money to support his musical passions, and you with your overly dramatic sensibility, would be a match.' Her aunt became red in the face, and Daisy looked around for help. Smithers was running toward them from the house with John following behind as quickly as he was able.

As if she was just aware of the commotion, Lady Beatrice abruptly came to herself. By the time the others were with them, she was in command of her emotions and rose to her feet. 'Forgive me, Mr Brent. I am unused to making do without Elspeth's assistance in the mornings. Perhaps I will return to the breakfast parlour and drink another cup of Cook's excellent chocolate. Smithers, you may attend me.' Daisy caught

Smithers's startled glance and wondered briefly about protesting.

'Of course, if your mistress is in need of you, then I will summon one of the undermaids.' Lady Beatrice managed to imbue her words with sufficient accusation that Daisy had to relent.

'I am sure Smithers will be able to help you with your morning's occupation, ma'am,' Daisy replied.

'Good. I shall be indebted to her for a first-hand explanation of how my daughter's wardrobe fell into a tub of bleach.' Too late, Daisy realised she'd allowed Smithers to be caught up in an inquisition.

'As to that, Lady Beatrice,' John interrupted, 'you will remember from childhood forays how narrow the passage is outside the housekeeper's room?'

Lady Beatrice nodded with a little reluctance.

'And so the accident is easily explained. Smithers was carrying all the dresses out to air them in the yard, when she was charged by the boot boy, and her bundles fell from her grasp. She was beside the alcove housing the great wooden tub of bleach. Inescapable,' John concluded his monologue.

Daisy dropped her eyes to see a beetle crawling through the grass at her feet. Light reflected on its scales and flashed shards of green. Such beauty, and so unexpected. 'We are very sorry, Aunt Beatrice, but Toby has made good the loss, you know,' she said calmly.

'As well he might. Has the boot boy been discharged?'

'No, ma'am. I cannot think Stephens will discharge him for escaping a swarm of bees.' Daisy knew there had been such a swarm yesterday because one or two of the staff had been stung. The gardeners had spent some time recovering it and setting a new bole. She hoped the boot boy would have been rushing around. Boot boys usually did, and John seemed very confident in his tale.

'I can see everything is understandable,' Lady Beatrice said, making it quite clear she thought she was being hoodwinked. 'Come, Smithers. If there is no bleach around this morning, I would like you to alter the bodice of my best morning gown.'

Daisy and John watched the pair walk back to the house, and when they were out of earshot she turned to her betrothed.

'Tell me, John, why you are so well acquainted with the back passages and entrances to this house?'

* * *

Across town, Reuben was engaged on business for his lordship that would have been of great interest to both Daisy and Lady Beatrice had they but known of it. Having escorted his sister and Miss Elspeth Howie to visit the animals in the Exeter 'change, he'd taken them to meet his mama at Gunther's Tearooms before setting off for the docks.

Striding along the riverside, Reuben breathed in the smell of the Thames. At once rank with floating rubbish and fresh with the seaward breeze and its promise of foreign lands, the water lapped against the great stakes holding up the piers. The tide had ebbed, and Reuben reckoned he had two hours at most to find his quarry before all hands were confined to deck. Once the tide turned, the master of the *Leith Rose* would be anxious to make his way out into the throng of boats and downstream for the North Sea.

Reuben needed to interview the mate, one Alasdair Cummings Farquerson, before he sailed for Leith. This hour or so before departure Reuben believed to be the best time to find the man both sober and refreshed.

'Ahoy there!' he called up to the deck. The boat rose and fell rhythmically. 'Ahoy, *Leith Rose*! Is Farquerson aboard?'

'Who wants tae ken?'

'Longreach, Reuben Longreach.' Reuben scanned the sides of the ship and picked out several figures moving around among the barrels and swirls of rope and sails. The owner of the voice looked over the side, assessing him for a moment or two before disappearing into a hatch. Within minutes, he'd returned and shouted to Reuben.

'Ye're tae come awa' on board, Mister Longreach. The mate will see ye now.'

Reuben turned and signed to the Grosvenor Square footman he'd brought with him. The lad was big and burly, and Reuben wanted him seen and on the dock. He could escape back to the earl with the intelligence of Reuben's whereabouts should this interview go badly.

He scrambled across the gangplank and took a moment to right himself on the slippery planks of the deck. He was wondering about the wisdom of going below when Farquerson stuck his head out of the forward hatch and climbed nimbly onto the deck. He was a neat individual of around thirty, business-like in his movements, and alert to the activity around him. The crew would not be shirking with this man in charge. He was no drunkard either.

'It's the earl's cousin, I see,' Farquerson said with a small chuckle. 'Longreach would be the right name for all you tall gangly folk, I'm thinking. Come walk with me, Mr Longreach, and tell me why I'm honoured by two visits from the earl's relatives in one day.'

'Two?' Reuben said spontaneously, and realised immediately he would get no information at all if he showed his hand to be so weak.

'Aye, two, although Mr Howie is only by marriage and does not have the length or strength of the real thing.' Farquerson pressed his hand into the small of Reuben's back, urging him to move forward to a place where there were no bales or barrels that could conceal a man who wanted to hide. When they had taken up a position far enough from the bustle of the crew to suit the mate, he stopped and turned his weather-beaten face to Reuben. 'Now, Mr Longreach, what do you want from me?'

Reuben mulled over the question. Until the mate's revelation that Mr Howie had been onboard, he knew exactly what he wanted from him. Now he was less sure.

He tossed questions around in his head and took a decision.

'What I want from you, Mr Farquerson, is the name of Lady Beatrice Howie's agent in Edinburgh, if you would be so obliging, please?' Reuben saw it was the right question. Farquerson let a flash of disappointment escape in his gaze before he shuttered it.

'Aye, that would be Mr Angus MacAngus of Leith. He acts for her ladyship, and we have taken several consignments of goods from him to bring to London.'

'Several? The most recent being — ?' Reuben raised an eyebrow and watched the mate's changing expression. The man had not yet asked for any money, but Reuben was careful to dangle his hat in one hand while shifting a bag of coins around in his coat pocket. Toby had been abundantly clear in his instructions. They had done as much as they were able by themselves, and now they needed to engage the services of someone working for Lady Beatrice.

'Is that a nervous tic you have there, Mr Longreach, or is it a useful contribution to a man's drinking funds?'

'You are not a drinker, Mr Farquerson, despite the rumours circulating. Your eyes are not blood-shot and your hand is steady. However, his lordship is interested in reliable information and can be grateful.' Reuben was pleased the sally had struck home. Whatever Farquerson intended to do by selling out Lady Beatrice, it wasn't to drink himself into a stupor.

'I see you are observant, sir.' The mate moved across the deck and stared over the side into the swirling waters. He contemplated something for a moment or two before turning and coming back to Reuben. 'Do you ask why a man would serve twa maisters?'

'Why? He might have come to his senses and begin to understand that not all was as innocent as it seemed — that by not asking questions of the first master, collusion in wrong-doing was being established,' Reuben said.

'Fifty guineas.'

'I have it, Mr Farquerson.' Reuben set his hat on the deck between his feet and pulled the heavy bag from his pocket. He eased the strings and allowed Farquerson to study the moving pile of coins.

'Lady Beatrice sent a consignment of papers in a leather-bound trunk down with us last week,' Farquerson said calmly. 'The trunk was padlocked, but there are ways ...'

'Did you read any of these papers?'

'Why, and so I did, Mr Longreach. I would not want to find myself involved in sedition, now, would I?' The man spoke with infuriating insolence, and Reuben wondered if he'd lost him. The papers were long gone if Howie had been here this afternoon, and Farquerson could make up anything he wanted.

'They were written in fancy script and even fancier language. I would say they were legal documents. One or two of them were sealed, and it was not possible to read the contents without making it obvious a body had been there first.' The mate turned sharply and yelled at an unfortunate boy dangling from a rope above their heads.

Reuben held his breath until the lad was safely back onto the beam he'd been clambering along. How had Farquerson known he was in trouble?

'We lost one at sea on the voyage down. I canna afford to lose any more,' Farquerson said. The cynical observation chilled Reuben. 'The papers that weren't sealed might have been practice specimens, Mr Longreach. They were about a trust, the Wilmot trust. They appeared to me to be about how a body would break such a fund and secure the capital sums rather than continue to receive income.'

Reuben handed over the bag of guineas. The earl's fears were justified. Lady Beatrice was intent on breaking the trust that paid not only her inheritance, but Daisy's as well. Elspeth and any future females in the line would also be defrauded were she to succeed, because once the lands and bonds were sold off, no income would accrue. It must always seem attractive to a person short of cash to secure a capital sum. Lady Beatrice clearly wanted to go against the wishes of her grandmother's will, and Farquerson was right to be concerned. Colluding at such an act of dishonesty would have very serious implications for him were it known.

'Are you taking back anything to Mr Angus MacAngus?' Reuben asked, and watched the mate closely. The man kept his gaze steady while he replied.

'Not as yet.'

'I thought you sailed on this tide,' Reuben protested.

'I thought so, too, Mr Longreach, but I am missing my captain and I do not sail without him.' A hackney clattered across the boards of the dock, and the mate swung round to study it. 'I see it will be possible. Captain Elliot has arrived. He is expert at judging how long he may remain with his friends and still catch the tide.'

The captain's arrival had stirred the crew into frantic activity, and Reuben knew he had only a few precious seconds to ask the question Farquerson expected of him and he had been withholding.

'So, man, who is Lady Beatrice's London lawyer?'

'Why would I know that, sir?'

'Because you are the fool of no one, Mr Farquerson. I'll bet any stake you've followed Mr Howie's carriage.' Reuben threw the challenge down like a gauntlet.

'Aye, it's no' difficult given the pace a carriage has to travel at around these congested streets. If I'm to benefit his lordship and myself . . .'

Behind them the captain fell onto the deck, and time was running out. Reuben struggled to avoid raising expectations in Farquerson, but they needed his help in the coming weeks.

'His lordship will no doubt reward advance notice, as it should be prized.'

'Aye, his lordship will no doubt do so. Pemmican is the man's name. He is not of the first rank of lawyers as I understand it, but Mr Howie believes he has need of ready cash and will therefore sail a mite close to the wind. Pemmican — off Essex

Street, in the Yard.' Behind his mate, the captain rose from his knees and bellowed.

Reuben moved nimbly back along the rail and, with an elegant leap, cleared the deck. Farquerson tossed his hat after him, and the meeting was over.

9

Daisy had derived no very satisfactory answer from John on the question of how he knew so much about the layout of the Grosvenor Square house, but the answer she did receive was long. It was much longer than she wanted and referred to so many boyish scrapes and youthful indiscretions, she began to wonder when Toby and John had found time to join their schools, universities, or regiments. Eventually she excused herself to wait on her mama, and encouraged John to take the rest recommended by his physician.

'Daisy — I had thought you were whiling away the morning with Mr Brent. No matter. Anna and I would welcome assistance in choosing colours for the main rooms in the Dower House.' Lady Mellon and her companion were seated at a large table, and the whole surface was covered with pattern books and swatches of curtain materials. Daisy felt her spirits sink further.

'Is it a matter of urgency to redecorate the Dower House, Mama? Surely Mariah would welcome your support while she learns how to run a household of this size and complexity.' Daisy smiled at Anna and chose a seat across the table from them. She lifted some Indian cotton from the pile of materials and breathed in the dry leafy smell from it.

'No, it is not a matter of urgency, but where one has decided views on what one wants, there is no excuse for prevarication. While I am normally easy-going, I find I do have decided views about what colours I want on my walls and on my sofas. Now, do you think I may match this coral with deep red cushions?' Lady Mellon bent over the fabrics and Daisy tried to focus.

She was relieved to hear her mama's explanation, because it meant the spat with Toby had been resolved, and she was not determined to abandon Mariah to the enormous task of running Toby's houses without guidance.

'Should you be taxing your brain with Toby's ill humour, Daisy, please desist. He thought to interfere between me and my housekeeper when we understood one another perfectly. His intrusion only plays into Beatrice's hands, I fear.' Lady Mellon looked up, and Daisy saw her squint as light caught the tiny glass shards sewn into some of the Indian fabric, and it winked at her.

'And how did it do that?' Daisy asked, more sharply than she intended. 'We struggle to keep my aunt under any kind of control, even with Mrs Burtles's expert management, and yet you would have let her go?'

'I would only have let her go in name, my dear. She would have been below stairs running the house as usual,' Lady Mellon said calmly.

'Oh.'

'Indeed, oh. I fear men need to be seen to win every battle or challenge they take up. Where my sister-in-law is concerned, I am content to allow her to appear to have won, as long as my servants continue to answer to me.'

'And you were confident my aunt would have stayed above stairs?' Daisy asked in a mild protest, designed to retrieve some dignity for her absent brother.

'These things can be arranged,' Lady Mellon said enigmatically. 'Now, my dear Daisy, how was your morning with Mr Brent? Does he live up to your expectations of a betrothed?'

Daisy clutched the swatch of material she was holding and glanced enquiringly at her mama, but Lady Mellon had dropped her head again and was teasing the pleats from the Indian cotton. She felt unsure about her mama's question because it sounded as if the lady was suppressing amusement.

'John is most attentive, and when my aunt was overcome by agitation, he went off promptly to find assistance and came back with Smithers,' Daisy said. Her mama was bound to learn of the scene in the garden. There were so many relatives staying in the house, someone would have been loitering in the shrubbery.

'Did he? Did Beatrice have more than a nominal excuse for her vapours?'

'No, I think not, Mama,' Daisy lied. If Reuben were to press his attentions on her more closely then she would need her mama's support; but in view of her hopes of attaching Elspeth's affections for him, this was not going to happen.

'And how did Mr Brent fail in his role, my dear?'

Daisy met her mama's gaze and saw the concern there. How had she guessed?

'I do not say he fails as a betrothed, but he does take an inordinate interest in the gossip of the house. I gave him every opportunity to admire my new gown with these beautiful emerald inserts, and he did not do so.' Anna clucked sympathetically and Daisy glanced her way. 'Yes, it was you who pointed out the design to me, Anna. I am disappointed John did not see how effective they are.' Daisy sat back and closed her eyes. She heard more clucking and a soft exchange in Spanish between the others. Her tired brain was unequal to the task of translating.

'I think Mr Brent has ordered his carriage for this afternoon,' her mama said. 'If Elspeth has returned by then, you might be able to prise her away from your aunt to give some countenance to your expedition. If not, I will be content for you to take Smithers.'

Daisy's eyes flew open. 'I am not aware of an expedition.'

'No, my dear? Mr Brent may be of the opinion he now commands your time.'

Daisy stared at her mama's bland expression. How had this come about? Did every lady give up the management of her life to her betrothed? Daisy bridled.

* * *

'I wonder whether Lady Mellon is at home, Stephens?'

Daisy heard Reuben's confident tones float across the downstairs hall as she began to descend towards the front door. Reuben stood in a cluster with Mrs Longreach, his mama, and Charlotte.

Daisy knew Elspeth had returned earlier because she'd heard Mrs Howie forbidding her luncheon on the grounds she'd been indulged beyond anything reasonable at Gunther's. The woman was able to poison even the blandest outing in very few words.

'Good afternoon, ma'am,' she said to Mrs Longreach, and kissed the older lady warmly. 'Charlotte.'

'Why, Daisy, you look very grown-up,' Mrs Longreach said in surprise. 'I suppose it must be nearly four years since I was last in London.'

'Five, Mama, and you saw Daisy last night, did you not?' Reuben asked with good humour. Daisy saw his mama twinkle at the gentle teasing.

'Of course, but somehow there is more of an air of gravitas about a carriage dress than an evening ensemble.'

'You are going out?' Reuben addressed Daisy.

'Mr Brent feels able to endure a short carriage trip and has invited Elspeth and me to join him. He wishes to consult his tailor about the suitability of some cloth he brought back from the north two weeks ago.' Daisy cast a glance at Reuben and Charlotte. 'But perhaps you hoped to find Elspeth with my mama and the other Scottish ladies?'

'We did,' Charlotte replied for them all. 'But we were enlivened by her company this morning and so should give up the pleasure to you, Daisy.'

'Not so, sister,' Reuben said. 'Daisy and Mr Brent are spending the daytime hours today getting to know each other as sweethearts. You oblige them by seeking out Elspeth.'

Daisy quashed her disappointment. Truth to tell, she had been hoping to secure Elspeth's company before any of the others sought it. Being alone with John was not proving to be as stimulating as she had expected. However, if her cousin stayed at home, it was another opportunity for Reuben to discover Elspeth's excellent qualities.

'You must all join the ladies in the drawing-room,' she said. Behind her,

Stephens padded down the grand staircase, and she decided to anticipate his welcome from Lady Mellon. 'Mama has been busy with Anna this morning, but I think they are now ready to receive. I know how Elspeth values your conversation, Reuben.'

Daisy saw the tiny glance that passed between Charlotte and Mrs Longreach. It was clear to her that they had noticed how much attention Reuben was paying to Elspeth. If his mama and sister were to promote the match, it would make Daisy's job a great deal easier. Why then did she feel so deflated? There could be little truth in her aunt's suggestion that Reuben also wanted her for the family money. She knew she was the very last wife Reuben would want, money or no money.

'Alas, I am needed by the earl this afternoon,' Reuben said. 'I think, too, there will be much talk about dresses and hair ornaments and all things suitable for wedding arrangements.'

'That's more than likely, Reuben,' his mama said. 'However, I hope such female concerns are not entirely above your notice?'

'Not all of them, Mama. I do notice, for example, what a lovely gown my cousin is wearing today. Emerald green particularly suits your colouring, Daisy.' Reuben made a small bow to include them all and set off into the back of the house where Toby's study lay.

'He is in the right,' Charlotte said. 'Emerald green does set off the Longreach colouring to near perfection. Enjoy your outing, Daisy. I see Stephens waits to take us up.'

Daisy stood on as the others ascended, but her attention was drawn upwards by John's loud guffaw. He and Elspeth walked along the upper landing. Their heads were together, and when John glanced down and saw her, his expression became conscious — as if he'd been caught out discussing her.

'Daisy, my dear, I am sorry to keep you waiting. I was explaining to Elspeth how Draker put me on the trail of the bolts of cloth we take to the tailor today,'

John said as he came downstairs. His movements were still very careful, but he managed well enough. Elspeth came, too.

'It is most interesting, Daisy. I know John ... I mean, Mr Brent, will have explained it to you, but Draker seems to be an asset among servants.' Elspeth spoke rapidly, and blushed a little.

'Goodness, Elspeth, as John already uses your given name, I cannot see why you may not use his,' Daisy said. 'He will be one of the family before very long.'

She caught a glimpse of John's expression and saw confusion there. Was he even aware he'd taken to calling her cousin Elspeth?

'Quite, quite,' he muttered, and dropped the final tread or two onto the tiles. His boots gleamed, and he was wearing a diamond pin in his neck cloth. Even so, the bruising down the side of his face was still the first thing one's eye was drawn to, Daisy thought. It reminded her of how much she owed him.

'Reuben had hoped to spend the

afternoon with you, Elspeth, but Toby has a prior claim on his time. I do hope you will excuse him. Perhaps they will be finished with their tedious business, whatever it is, before his mama requires his escort back to change for dinner.'

The blush that stained Elspeth's cheeks then was most rewarding, and made up a little for the failure of her ploy to bring the distant cousins together. Daisy silently congratulated herself on her choice of wording. Reuben would not be able to contradict it. He would never hear of it.

What was the business he and Toby were contracting? she wondered. Of late, her brother had often found excuses to secure Reuben's company, and that was quite unusual. The two men were temperamentally different. A niggle of suspicion and unease entered her brain.

* * *

Daisy again settled back in a carriage, but she was less enthusiastic about this trip than she had been about taking Elspeth to Mademoiselle Juliette's salon. John fidgeted.

'Your discomfort reminds me of a wolf hound Papa was particularly fond of. It used to wriggle in just this fashion after it had been swimming in the river.' She sent John a challenging look, and he became still.

'I think you are severe, my dear Daisy. I am in discomfort, not to say pain, and would not be making this journey had I not discovered from Toby's man that my tailor is planning a holiday to visit his aged parents in Manchester.'

Daisy suppressed a squeal of exasperation. She knew John had lived with serious financial strictures for many years, but even so, his wardrobe was extensive. There was really no necessity for this excursion when his ribs still pained him, and she wanted to be back in Grosvenor Square discovering why her brother and Reuben were so close.

'Will Mr Preston not leave his senior cutter in charge of the workshop?'

'More than likely, but I cannot trust

my expensive cloth to underlings, however talented.' John flicked the cuffs of his shirt. 'You would not want to find yourself dealing with an apprentice at Mademoiselle Juliette's, now, would you?'

'No, but I know Mademoiselle does not do all the cutting and stitching herself. There would not be enough hours in the day.' Daisy heard Smithers stifle a sigh at her side. No doubt she could explain to John how long it took to make a lady's dress. She'd spent two hours working on the seams of Lady Beatrice's gown that morning.

'I hear you sigh, Smithers, and I know why. It was too bad of Lady Beatrice to spoil your morning,' John said sympathetically.

'Thank you, sir. I hope my services improved my lady's dress. She did say it felt more comfortable when I'd finished,' Smithers replied with the diplomacy that marked out a senior servant, but Daisy knew her maid had passed a difficult morning. Why was her aunt so much more demanding on this visit than on previous ones? she wondered.

'I expect you're wondering why Toby and Reuben are so much in each other's company at present,' John said conversationally as the carriage slowed to a halt outside the tailor's workshop. 'It's simply that Reuben will be playing the organ for his wedding, and they are unable to reach agreement over what voluntaries Reuben will offer. He has very decided views.'

Daisy gave John a long look full of speculation. Why did he throw that remark into the air as if he was tossing her a sweetmeat? Sudden understanding flooded her brain. The men were engaged in a conspiracy, and John was involved. He did not have to see his Mr Preston today, but it suited the others to have Daisy removed from Grosvenor Square.

She sat back against the squabs, lifting her head and narrowing her eyes. All three of the men in her life were working together to keep something from her. How could she find out what? She cleared her brow of the unbecoming wrinkles brought on by concentration. Of the three, John was the least able to keep a secret, and he was alone with her for the carriage drive home.

* * *

'Your help was most welcome, m'dear,' John said as the carriage lurched away from its stand. While the vehicle settled into a sedate roll, Daisy bided her time. There were several well-known bottle-necks on their route, and she could afford to tease the information she wanted from her betrothed rather than ask bluntly.

'I was a little surprised to hear you say Reuben and Toby were discussing the music for the earl's marriage ceremony,' she said at last.

Smithers caught a tightly wrapped parcel as it slid floorwards and held it on her lap. John had spent lavishly in the tailor's workshop, but eventually even he could see he would be returning most of his choices.

'This new paper they use is very shiny,' he said.

Daisy ignored the attempt to divert her attention. 'You did say it was music?' She kept her eyes fixed on John.

'Your eyes are the deepest chocolate colour, m'dear. I have noticed it before on occasion. What can have roused you in the tailor's workshop?' He wriggled in his corner, though whether from physical discomfort or an agitation of his nerves she was unable to decide.

'Oh, dissimulation, perhaps, John.' She allowed him a tiny smile. 'Are Toby and Reuben discussing music?'

'Yes, music.' John slipped his fingers inside the starched cotton of his neck cloth and eased its tightness. 'Toby and Mariah have the vaguest of ideas. He is not much used to anything other than military marches, and she ... ' He looked around the carriage, and Daisy wondered whether he expected to find some clue about Miss Fox's musical tastes etched into its faded velvet trappings. 'She is usually reading, I find.'

Smithers coughed, and Daisy was aware of the maid pulling a handkerchief from her pocket to suppress it. She would have laughed, had it not seemed more prudent to let John think she believed this nonsense.

'Usually reading?' Daisy parroted with the very slightest of inflections. 'I know Mariah has spent a lot of time absorbing educational materials, but I do think she has a great social veneer. You told me yourself how well she coped during her first encounter with Sir Lucas Wellwood.'

'I did, indeed I did. She coped remarkably well, but she does not have the sophisticated command of a musical repertoire demanded by your cousin,' John gabbled, and Daisy was almost moved to pity him.

'Do Reuben and Toby discuss anything other than music?' she asked rather more boldly than she had anticipated, but the carriage was making exceptional progress.

'No!' John's eyes bulged and his complexion fired. 'No, they are entirely focused on music. Why, Toby does not know Reuben was at the docks.'

Daisy was silenced. She saw the panic flash of realisation light John's eyes before he closed them and gave a small groan. He should not have said that, she thought as he clutched his side.

'I am in pain again, m'love. I may ramble a bit as a result,' John said, and added a moan Daisy might have thought theatrical in other circumstances.

'I am so sorry to hear that, John. We will be at Grosvenor Square instantly, and Draker will be able to have a hot bath drawn for you.'

'My love.' John opened his eyes. 'You are the very kindest betrothed a man could have. I count myself to be very fortunate.'

Daisy wondered whether John would feel so fortunate once Toby discovered how much he'd given away.

10

'He has gone to the stables,' Reuben said.

Daisy stood still in the shadow of the suit of armour that guarded Toby's study door. How had Reuben spotted her there? she wondered. Did one of her feet protrude beyond the metal? Did she cast a shadow herself?

'Your perfume is most distinctive. It wafts on the summer air and attracted my attention,' he said in answer to her unasked question.

'Yes, Stephens likes to keep windows open in the lower reaches of the house. The result is sometimes a stiff breeze.' She stepped forward. 'I will take more care lest my aunt shows similar qualities of detection.'

'Why are you lurking in the shadows, my dear? Surely you are not afraid to enter Toby's study?'

'I was not attempting to enter Toby's

study, as I was of the impression you and he were closeted discussing matters of great importance,' she said tartly. She tugged at the lace trim of her dress and, once it was satisfactorily flat, lifted her eyes to Reuben's. 'I saw my aunt approach the bottom of the staircase and I took refuge here.'

Reuben studied her, his gaze now by no means relaxed, and its normal thin layer of merriment absent from his demeanour. Daisy thought she detected lines of strain around the deep-set Longreach eyes.

'Refuge? Because Toby is the one person who awes Lady Beatrice?' Reuben asked, and Daisy nodded. She had not realised the truth of this observation until Reuben made it. Lady Beatrice was afraid of Toby, or of the power Toby represented.

'As you know, I have been to John's tailor with him,' she said, and Reuben raised an eyebrow. 'It seems that Perkins had learned Mr Preston intended to make an extended visit to his parents in

Manchester; however, this is not true.'

'Ah,' Reuben said.

'Ah, indeed.'

'I am expected in the drawing-room to escort Mama and Charlotte back to our lodgings, although your mama has once more offered her hospitality this evening.' Reuben stood away, leaving space for Daisy to precede him along the corridor. Mutinously, she remained where she was.

'I will hope to see you at dinner, my dear, if Smithers can awake you from this stasis.'

'Reuben, why were you at the docks?'

'Who says I've been at the docks?'

'I wish some member of this family would allow of my natural intelligence,' Daisy snapped. 'I have spent two woefully wasted hours in a carriage and tailor's workshop with John. How would I not discover it was a ruse to remove me from here?'

'No one denies your intelligence, but it would be advisable to forget Mr Brent's indiscretion, in particular in the hearing of your aunt and her husband.'

'That, sir, simply demonstrates my meaning.' Daisy would have moved then, and had turned towards the front of the house, but Reuben stepped closer and she was trapped against the wall. They were concealed from the traffic in the main hall by the armour of her long-dead ancestor. She looked up into a severe expression, and might have quailed were it not for the huge bubble of anger brewing in her.

Seconds ticked away on the faces of the hall clocks while Reuben stared down at her. She saw a tic work in the muscle above his jaw and knew a perverse degree of triumph. Perhaps she had not learned why the man was among the docks, but she had unsettled his normal arrogant composure.

'I was not at the docks, Daisy,' Reuben said finally.

She bit the inside of her cheek to prevent a protest escaping.

'I am sure Mr Brent invented a story to cover up my actual destination. I was visiting a lady.'

Heat curled in Daisy's stomach and she brought a hand to her mouth. Reuben *did* have a mistress!

'Why should John not tell me you were visiting a lady? Unless, of course, she is not.'

Reuben straightened, and his full height made him every bit as intimidating as Toby in a temper.

'You are out of your depth discussing a gentleman's friends. However, I saw the expression you wore yesterday when you thought Charlotte was one such. Were you not betrothed to the estimable Mr Brent, I might have been well pleased with it.' Reuben smoothed the front of his waistcoat, and she watched his long fingers caress the watch chain lying across his ribs.

'How dare you make such an assertion?' she asked, allowing her anger to colour her voice and bring unwanted heat to her cheeks. 'Mr Brent is everything I might desire in a betrothed.'

'I'm sure of it,' Reuben replied briskly. 'And should your union be often blessed, he will ably run the house without bringing in one of his sisters.'

Daisy felt the blood rush through her ears, and a chill brought goose-bumps across her skin. It was one of the matters that troubled her most when considering the married state. At not quite nineteen, she did not relish believing only motherhood lay in front of her.

'It is true John interests himself in the running of the house, but I am convinced he will soon find other outlets when the coal business is fully operational,' she said, ignoring the challenge Reuben was throwing at her.

'You, Daisy, are worth so much more than to be a brood mare for John Brent.'

Daisy lifted her hand and brought it hard across Reuben's cheek. She felt the strength of his hands when he gripped her upper arms and dragged her hard against him. Fire flashed in his eyes.

'Such a challenge will not go unpunished, my dear,' he said at last, and she heard the effort to be restrained behind his words. She felt the power ease from his muscles as he let her go and stepped away. 'In the meantime, remember I was with a lady this afternoon. A matter best not discussed in your mama's drawing-room.'

* * *

Reuben escorted his mama and Charlotte back to their lodgings; once he heard the door of their suite close, he left the building again. Should they ask, he would make up some story about collecting fresh tobacco or ordering wine. Anything would do, because his mama and his sister were not suspicious of his actions. Daisy, on the other hand, was alerted.

He'd left a note for Toby, warning him that Daisy was in possession of half a story. Half a story was much more dangerous than no story, or even the full tale of her aunt's wickedness as they had so far established it. Reuben was shaken to the core.

Why had Toby insisted on soliciting help from Brent? Reuben groaned aloud, causing two ladies walking towards him to step sideways. John Brent was one of the worst gossips he had ever met, and at present he was also befuddled by the amount of laudanum and alcohol he was consuming to dull his pain. Yet Toby regarded Brent as his best friend, and would hear no counter-suggestion.

Reuben stopped. He took several deep breaths and began walking again with just as much purpose, but more slowly. He turned the corner and hailed a hackney cab.

'Essex Street,' he called up to the driver. 'Stop before the entrance to the Yard.' He settled into the dank interior. Howie had not returned to the house after his visit to the *Leith Rose*, and both Reuben and Toby decided it would suit them well to reconnoitre the premises of the errant lawyer. Toby could not be spared, and so the work fell to Reuben.

As the horse clipped onwards, Reuben gazed out onto the passing crowds. How many of them were involved in grasping and cheating to stay alive and out of the debtors' prison? What had gone wrong in the Howies' lives to put them in the desperate straits they found themselves combating? Reuben sighed.

'Longreach.' Reuben heard Edward Howie's Scottish brogue address him. He knocked on the roof of the cab and it came to a standstill. The older man studied him from the pavement, and Reuben knew he would have to exchange compliments with him at the very least. He descended and called back to the driver to wait as he stepped away from the hackney.

'Mr Howie. Good evening, sir.' He schooled his expression into mild surprise before he lifted his head. Howie was accompanied by a tall individual whose unhealthy pallor betrayed ill health, or addiction, and whose clothes suggested he was the lawyer, Pemmican.

'I had not thought to find you driving away from the fashionable part of town. Surely there are no pipe organs worthy of your skills down towards the docks?' Howie asked.

Reuben saw the speculative gleam in the man's close-set eyes and realised he was alert to the possibilities that might be taking Reuben to the unsavoury courts and passages surrounding the docks. The Howies were so immersed in their objective of breaking the trust that he and Toby had hoped they were unmindful of the interest of others in their affairs. It was clear now to Reuben that they had miscalculated.

'Not pipe organs, sir, no. I am heading out on a more delicate mission for an old friend,' Reuben said, and he hoped it would be enough to deflect Howie's suspicions.

'Ah yes, missions for friends lead many a young man into places where he might be best advised not to penetrate,' Howie observed. His companion shuffled at his side and scraped the rubbish-strewn pavement with the tip of a ragged umbrella. 'I used to indulge in such activities myself.'

'Really,' Reuben said, and he wondered whether he should ask what Howie had been doing there tonight. 'I imagine the young men of Edinburgh are every bit as adventurous and devil-may-care as their counterparts in London. However, you are in company, sir, and I surmise you have been tracking down a mill or a cock-fight?' He raised an eyebrow in quizzical but friendly enquiry, saw the calculating flash of understanding light Howie's expression, and hoped he'd done enough to deflect him.

'Not tonight, Longreach. I have been consulting my wife's London lawyer, Mr Albert Pemmican. Let me make him known to you.' Howie half-turned to the tall man and brought him forward. The individual made a small bow, which Reuben returned.

'Good evening, Mr Longreach,' Pemmican said in a deep bass voice that caught Reuben by surprise. 'I have a certain expertise in affairs that bring distress to young gentlemen and their families. If I can offer any professional help, sir, I would be delighted to consult with you.' He probed long fingers into a pocket of his coat and brought out a small square of card which he pressed on Reuben. 'My directions.' He made another infinitesimal bow and walked forward, leaving Reuben and Howie alone.

'I must follow him, Longreach,' Howie said. 'We have not yet concluded our discussions.' He made a polite bow. 'The docks are truly not a salubrious part of the city. You would be well advised not to stray there alone.'

Reuben heard the veiled threat and understood it. Howie was not fooled by his hinted diversion about the affairs of friends.

'And yet you walked alone there yourself?' he challenged.

'No,' Howie said, and Reuben caught sight of a large man lounging against a doorway. As Howie lifted his hand, the man peeled away and moved forward towards them. It was the Howies' coachman, Conor. He held a cudgel flat against his leg. 'No, Mr Longreach, I do not move around alone.'

11

Daisy watched the guests assemble in the drawing-room from a position of considerable social strength. John Brent was at her right shoulder and Elspeth Howie a little to her left. They chatted amiably with Daisy's relatives as Stephens directed the footmen around the room bearing trays of drinks.

'My love, if you will excuse me for a few moments, I need to speak with Toby,' John said, and without waiting for her response, he left Daisy and Elspeth unprotected. They caught a glimpse of his tall figure squeezing between Aunt Mathilde and Lady Beatrice, and then he was gone.

'My goodness, Daisy, John was most abrupt. He has been a little agitated since his trip to the tailor's. Did it not go well?' Elspeth asked.

'Well enough, I suppose,' Daisy replied.

'He was measured for a coat. He has already been with Toby. What can be occupying their attention quite so much?'

'Good evening, niece,' Lady Beatrice said.

Daisy's stomach muscles clenched. She nodded politely to her aunt, and would have moved away, but the woman set a hand on her arm.

'I would have a word, if you please. Elspeth, attend to your grandmamma.'

'What may I help you with, ma'am?' Daisy asked in a neutral tone as her cousin moved away.

'I am of the opinion that this marriage between the earl and Miss Fox is not in the best interests of the family. Do not bridle. The girl is well enough connected, but woefully over-educated.'

Daisy struggled to keep her temper in check and saw Elspeth's colour flare as she spoke with Mrs Howie. Was the older woman making the same argument? 'My brother is well into his majority, Aunt Beatrice. I cannot think he has not considered Miss Fox's family and character from every possible angle,' she said finally.

'Nonsense. It would be far more fitting for Toby to strengthen the family by marrying Elspeth. You must agree.' Lady Beatrice emphasised her point by tapping Daisy's forearm with her fan.

'I have always found it is unproductive to tell Daisy she must do anything, Lady Beatrice,' Reuben said at Daisy's elbow.

He had entered the room from the small anteroom and not the grand staircase, Daisy thought, even as her aunt snapped open the fan and waved it energetically in front of her face.

'Mr Longreach, I protest. I am engaged in a private conversation with my niece, and you insert your person where it is neither wanted nor needed,' she said in rising accents.

Daisy saw Mrs Howie detach herself from Elspeth and begin to move across the room towards them.

'I intend to tell Constanzia to have you barred from the house,' Lady Beatrice hissed at Reuben.

'Beatrice,' Mrs Howie said as she at last arrived beside them, 'I wonder if you would help me find Edward. I have not heard how his expedition in the late afternoon went.'

Lady Beatrice was clearly torn between her frustration at losing Daisy's undivided attention and obeying her mama-in-law's thinly veiled warning over her loudness. She watched with considerable interest as the older woman prevailed, and Lady Beatrice went off with her. As Elspeth was detained by an elderly uncle from the Newcastle area who had been standing close to the fireplace, Daisy found herself alone with Reuben.

'The room is crowded, my dear. I am protected from further assault,' he said with that infuriating prescience of her thoughts he displayed. 'And you are safe from retribution — at present.'

'How dare you approach me?' She curled the fingers of her right hand into her palm as if the pain would help her concentrate on the here and now and dispel the memory of the white-hot fury that had made her lash out. It was no concern of hers if Reuben kept thirty mistresses. 'There is a circle of bruises around each of my arms.'

She saw his glance drop to the thick silk shawl she wore draped across her upper arms. In truth, the bruises were faint, and Smithers had not remarked on them, but Daisy knew they were there.

'Unlike your aunt, you have serious grounds for asking your mama to debar me — and yet Stephens welcomed me with a glass of Toby's best champagne.' Reuben put a hand below her elbow and urged her towards the doors leading into one of the anterooms. 'Don't be miss-ish, Daisy. I must speak to you.'

She dug the small wooden heels of her evening shoes into the carpet, and Reuben was forced to stay still. 'I will not be alone with you, Reuben. You have betrayed my brother's trust ...'

'What's this?' Edward Howie asked, at such close quarters Daisy wondered if he had heard her remark. 'I have narrowly avoided a confrontation with my wife and my mama, and now I find you young people locked in combat.'

Reuben released her elbow, but it did not lend Daisy the comfort she expected. Being rescued by Mr Howie was nothing short of offering a hostage to her future prospects.

'No such thing, Uncle Edward. Reuben and I are wont to argue rather forcibly. It goes back to the rivalries of our childhood,' she said, and smiled, although she knew it was not in her eyes.

The older man drank deeply and snapped his fingers towards Matt. When he'd been relieved of the empty glass and furnished with another one brimming with fizzing wine, he too smiled. Daisy felt a chill creep across the skin of her shoulders and tense the muscles of her arms.

'Perhaps Mr Longreach will tell you what he was doing driving away from the respectability of his lodgings this afternoon. I was obliged to warn him of the nature of those streets one drives into very quickly.'

Daisy's heart jolted. The air around

them was alive with sparking tension. 'Reuben is familiar with most of London and of the City, sir. I don't think he needs your advice on what areas are safe to drive in or even walk around, but it was thoughtful of you to make the observation.'

'It was, Daisy. I have often said to Mr Pemmican, your aunt's lawyer, that he would have a larger and wealthier clientele if he would but move to another area — more fashionable, or simply further from the docks.' Mr Howie swirled the contents of his glass before he swallowed them in one gulp. 'However, he tells me he has had his premises for so many years that he cannot envisage making a change.'

'Making changes can be painful,' Daisy said, although she had the feeling this conversation existed on another level — a level only Reuben and her uncle understood.

'Indeed, they can cause pain. Afterwards, though, the body may be stronger,' Mr Howie said before walking away.

'His gait is a little unsteady,' Reuben

observed. 'Perhaps he has enjoyed more than a glass or two of champagne.'

'What was that about?' Daisy asked baldly, ignoring his attempt to divert her. 'Do you have business with my aunt's lawyer?'

'I think you look a little pale, Daisy. Possibly the after-effects of your disordered digestion are not quite cleared up,' Reuben said, but she heard the inflection lift his voice in a questioning tone. He had tilted his head and was moving closer to her, sliding an arm behind her back as he would were she in danger of fainting.

'What are you doing?' Daisy felt the smooth leather of Reuben's patent slipper caress the back of her right calf muscle before he jabbed her sharply in the left ankle. Now she was falling, if not fainting, and his strong arms lifted her from the floor.

'Scream if you will, Daisy,' he challenged with the mocking smile of their childhood, reminding her of more than one adventure she would rather forget.

'There's only one sure way to silence a woman in your position.'

Daisy closed her eyes. This was not the moment to have Reuben disgrace them both by kissing her.

* * *

Reuben knew Matt had set his tray aside and was slipping through the assembled relatives towards the door of the rose anteroom. Good man, he thought as the lad opened the door and stood aside to let Reuben and his drooping bundle pass through. He heard the door clip shut and set Daisy on her feet.

She sank onto a long stool and rubbed her ankle through the layers of her skirts. He waited. After a moment or two, her hand stilled and her head came up. Fire and ice flashed in the brilliant eyes, and Reuben admired the courage she displayed.

'How easy it would be to kidnap me,' she said. 'My relatives are so comfortable enjoying Toby's hospitality, they paid scant attention to your manoeuvre.'

'Had you wanted our departure noticed by anyone other than Matt, I have little doubt you would have succeeded.'

'Why are we here?'

'*You* are here because curiosity overcame your sense of self-preservation,' Reuben said calmly. '*We* are here because we await Toby's arrival.'

He saw her shoulders tense and knew a momentary pang of remorse. Daisy's life was about to change forever. Just when he would have spoken a word of comfort, the door onto the landing opened and Toby strode through. Reuben caught a brief glimpse of John Brent hurrying towards the drawing-room before the earl closed the door.

'Thank you, Reuben,' Toby said, crossing the floor and pulling Daisy up from her stool. 'My dear, I am conscious of how hard you have been worked in looking after our visitors, and I believe you would benefit from a day or two away from the throng.'

'What can you mean, Toby? If you

think I should go out to Richmond with you and Mariah, then you must put it out of your mind. We cannot leave Mama on her own to deal with Aunt Beatrice.'

Reuben was surprised by the quick flush of colour staining Daisy's cheeks. Perhaps his plan of forcing her into Brent's company had worked better than now suited their purposes.

'No? I am of the opinion Mama deals with Aunt Beatrice much more effectively than I do,' Toby said, and Reuben heard the weariness of his reply. It must be very hard to have to run the estates, defend one's name against a murder charge, and deal with domestic disharmony. However, their present aim was to remove Daisy from the house, where she was in serious danger of using her sharp intelligence to the wrong ends.

'Mr Brent goes this evening, I believe?' he asked the earl, and Toby nodded.

'Before dinner; he is taking leave of Mama as we speak. Daisy, I would really appreciate your presence in Richmond. Mariah and I have had so little conversation this past week, and were you to join the party we could occasionally slip away without John's sisters feeling bereft.'

'That is fustian, Toby.'

'As you wish, Daisy.' Toby clipped the words, and Reuben saw again the army officer who was never far below his powerful cousin's veneer of respectability. 'It is now an order. Smithers is packing, and you will leave tomorrow at ten in Aunt Mathilde's yellow carriage. Mama will take the town carriage to make a call on Mr Fox, and I will follow her in my curricle. Mariah will accompany me to Richmond.'

Daisy all but stamped her foot, but Reuben was not deceived. She was mutinous. While the men waited, she crossed the room and threw open the door onto the landing. Without another word, she left them.

He glanced at his cousin and felt the warmth of his stare in return. That, too, was an order. He had to make sure Daisy arrived in Richmond tomorrow.

Reuben dropped his eyes and studied

the stitching along the tops of his evening pumps. What he really wanted to do was tell Daisy how bad things were and give her the chance to act accordingly. For all that Toby was marrying a woman of education and strong mind, he did not see beyond the drama of Daisy's daily round. It was going to cause trouble for all of them. He felt it.

'Perhaps she would be less excitable if we laid the issues before her,' he said at last.

'Really?' Toby moved distractedly. Reuben wondered if his love for Mariah Fox was so intense that it blinded him to the damage Daisy was suffering by being treated like a child.

'She has a cool head. I have seen how she reacts to Lady Beatrice and Mrs Howie. If we continue to tell her what she must do, then I fear we will have an unexpected start on our hands.'

'Now you use the language of the horse, Reuben. I agree my sister is unsettled by Mariah's arrival in the family. I have watched with some interest as she realises life holds more than the Season. But her understanding is untutored. We do not have time to give her a sheaf of complex facts and expect her to act rationally.'

'I know Miss Fox went off after Lucas . . . '

'Exactly.' Toby was now running his fingers around the constricting neck cloth Perkins had wound so carefully. 'She will attempt to emulate Mariah's behaviour. I so nearly lost both of them.'

'Of course, sir.'

'I am sorry, Reuben. Sorry that you need to call me *sir*. I'm sorry that I need to be so forceful. I am sorry my aunt has caused this problem. But I do appreciate all you have done on behalf of the family, and I will not forget it.'

Reuben shifted his weight from one foot and back. He looked into the earl's face and realised there was no further reasoning with him then. Cool and intelligent soldier as he was, he had been pushed into a corner. Reuben would have to act alone where Daisy was concerned, because he was sure she would not follow brotherly orders without causing mayhem along the way.

* * *

'The earl believes I need to accompany him to Richmond and recuperate from the exertions of dealing with Lady Beatrice,' Daisy said that evening when Smithers had helped her into her night clothes and was brushing out the tangles from her long fall of hair.

'So he has said, my lady. I have packed for two nights, as I think we need to return early on Thursday in order to dress you and Miss Elspeth for the ball.'

Daisy watched her maid work through the glass and tried to calm her tumbling thoughts. The long hair was tamed and braided before she made much progress, however.

'I do not think the earl wants my company in Richmond. I think he and Mr Reuben want me out of Grosvenor

Square.' Daisy watched Smithers closely. Senior servants often knew far more about the undercurrents of life in a stately home than the family knew of one another. She was rewarded by a slight tug of her braid as the maid tried to tidy a few loose strands of hair.

'Mr Stephens has told Mrs Burtles that Mr Reuben will be occupying a room in Lord Mellon's wing while the earl is away, my lady. He said this was to offer assistance to Lady Mellon while you and the earl are both in Richmond.'

'Smithers, I do not think you have told me all you might,' Daisy said. She saw the tiny blush that tinged the woman's cheeks.

'I am sorry, my lady; the men are often closeted together, and Mr Stephens has engaged a new footman who has no household skills. I think you may be right. The earl does want you out of the house. He lost his temper with Mr Brent earlier this evening, and that was when Mr Reuben came to ask me to pack for a visit to Richmond.'

'Really?' Daisy asked, and quailed as the maid nodded. Their eyes met in the mirror, and she struggled to understand the import of everything Smithers said. 'Toby shouted at John?'

'The earl's footman was carrying away his washing water, my lady, when Mr Brent arrived in a hurry; and whatever it was he said, the earl was furious.' Smithers made a great play of folding the remaining bits of linen.

'Tell me,' Daisy said.

'Mr Reuben was already there, and Mr Perkins and the new footman —'

'Who isn't really a footman,' Daisy interrupted.

'No, he isn't. Mrs Burtles reckons he's one of them that investigates criminals.'

'Goodness, Smithers. What is going on in this family?'

'Mr Brent was saying as how he hadn't meant to say anything, but the earl must know how deuced — sorry, my lady — how deuced difficult it was to keep things from Daisy when she had a mind to learn them. Then the new footman closed the door, my lady.'

Daisy sat up straighter on her stool. So, she thought, Toby *did* want to keep things away from her, and John had let slip to her about Reuben being at the docks. And Reuben was driving away from town. She'd learned that from her uncle when he was clearly warning Reuben off going somewhere. Or — she bit her lip in agitation — was he telling Reuben he knew where he was going? Did Reuben need advice from the much-mentioned Mr Pemmican?

It was all very puzzling, but the end result for the present was that Toby wanted her in Richmond under John's eye. Daisy bridled. John would attach himself to her side and suffocate her with attention and conversation. It could hardly be borne.

'Where can we arrange to have the under-coachman break an axle?' she asked the startled maid.

'My lady?'

'I will not be trapped in Richmond for two days listening to Mr Brent expound his theories of household management.'

'But my lady, when you become Mrs Brent you will spend all your days with him in Richmond,' Smithers said.

Daisy raised stricken eyes to her maid's homely face. The woman's expression was full of concern, and it was nearly her undoing. How could she have allowed her purpose to wander to the extent that she was criticising John?

'Of course, Smithers, but that will be different. I will be a wife then, and wives have certain entitlements.' She stood up. 'I do not mean to criticise Mr Brent's preoccupation with the running of this house. It is simply that my papa was not in the least bit interested in domestic matters, and I do find it strange in Mr Brent.'

'The older servants speak well of your papa, my lady.' Smithers moved quietly around the bedroom. 'Will that be all, my lady?'

'Thank you, Smithers.'

Daisy sat by her fire while the household settled. She heard the house's doors opening and closing as her relatives retired to their suites. Footsteps padded down the corridor outside her room as the servants withdrew from the front premises, and the door onto the service stair clipped shut. Fifteen times she heard that door clip shut before there came a gap of twenty minutes when no one passed along.

She dived into the recesses of a large cupboard and emerged with a suit of clothes that had been her costume for a masque last Christmas. Velveteen trousers and a shirt and jacket of sorts were hardly what a stable boy wore, but they were much easier to move in when your purpose was to crawl around below a carriage.

12

The damp chill of evening dew hung around Reuben's ankles as he sat on a bollard to pull his boots on. He lifted his dress shoes from the mud and stuffed them into the outside pocket of his caped riding coat before turning abruptly towards the sound of approaching feet.

Sliding into the first open door in the mews, he watched a drunken groom lurch along the central channel of the cobbled lane. He narrowed his eyes in concentration, but the man was certainly what he appeared to be. Further along, and two stable boys scampered out to assist him onto an outside stair. They all disappeared into a hay loft.

Reuben breathed deeply. The moon was up, and the resulting light made everything indistinct and ghostly. An owl hooted mournfully from the square. He shifted his weight and listened again. Was it an owl, or was it one of Howie's thugs?

The earl was nowhere to be seen, but Reuben knew he was secreted among the horses with Matt and Josh, a younger boy brought back from the Fox household in Redde Place. John Brent's carriage would by now be skirting the Royal Park and drawing towards his house in Richmond with Brent, Draker and Miss Fox's maid, Tilly. Reuben wished Daisy and her maid had gone with them. Maybe the earl was correct in his approach. Maybe Daisy would be safer out of the firing line.

A creak alerted him to another person moving around. The back gate from the townhouse was deep in shadows, but he thought a line of less dense blackness was discernible, even in the moonlight. Would Howie himself come through that way? Surely they were expecting invaders rather than escapees?

As Reuben watched, the line thickened until a slight shadow shivered through the gateway and pulled it closed behind him. The shadow was not Howie. It was too small.

He muttered several curses. Daisy! Daisy was wandering around the mews. The damp summer night would mute her footsteps. But they'd see her, and she was a much more attractive prospect as a hostage than the Scottish girl. Easier to remove, as she was already out of the house, and worth more to ransom, being the earl's sister.

Reuben tensed. Toby and the other men scattered through the mews were too distant to call to. Stamford, the investigator, and several of his associates were hiding behind trees in the square. Their plan was to converge behind the interlopers when they came and cut them off in the back garden. Now Daisy was out of the garden and into the mews that ran left and right. The buildings had myriad doors and outside stairways. The gardens of the other great houses had gateways. There was no possibility of ensuring her safety except by taking her first. He would have to lift her and remove her.

* * *

Daisy thought she heard movement along the mews lane and stood still, listening intently. An owl had sounded as she crossed the last bit of lawn before reaching the gate into the mews. The gate was cumbersome, and it creaked so loudly to her ears that she thought everyone must hear it in the servants' hall and come out to investigate.

No one came. The night settled into damp moonlit eeriness. She peeled herself from the safety of the gate and fixed her gaze on the huge doors across the carriage house. They were moved along the wall on oiled rollers, and she knew James would have padlocked them tonight. With so many required tomorrow and for the earl's wedding on Friday, he wouldn't be taking any risks with the vehicles.

Daisy also knew there was a way into the loft from the tack room of the neighbouring stable. She heard the familiar shuffling of the carriage horses, but no human sounds. The men would be asleep in their own corners. She relied on that to allow her to sabotage the carriage.

Once across the cobbled lane, she eased open the tack room door and slid through. The blackness of night was dense inside, and Daisy stopped to let her eyes adjust. A thin stream of moonlight penetrated an astragal and revealed a rickety wooden stair directly ahead. She set one foot on the first step but paused. She would need a tool to loosen the bolts, or whatever she could loosen beneath the floor of the carriage Toby had assigned to take her to Richmond.

It was as she turned towards the bench of the tack room that disaster struck. A hand came across her mouth and a strong arm around her waist. She struggled free, but fell over something discarded on the floor, tumbling towards the edge of the stairs. Daisy cracked her head and slid into a darkness blacker than that of the moonlit stable.

* * *

'You're awake,' Reuben said.

Daisy blinked in the strong morning light. She felt sure she'd been awake already, perhaps more than once. Across the room, Reuben Longreach sat in an armchair and studied her with the intensity he usually reserved for something particular.

'Why do you gaze at me as if I were one of your fragile rolls of organ music?'

In a different and smaller chair, a woman sat with sewing on her lap. She rose when Daisy spoke, and cast Reuben an enquiring glance. Daisy saw irritation there. Although her demeanour was not that of a servant, the lady crossed to a wash-stand, where she wrung out a cloth in water. Daisy watched the stream of liquid fall back into the basin and realised she was very thirsty.

The lady came near to the bed Daisy lay on and gently dabbed her forehead. 'Oh, that hurts,' she moaned. Her head ached, and for a moment or two her vision was clouded. The lady stepped back.

'Sorry, Lady Daisy, but the doctor said

to keep cleaning the wound.' She moved away, and Daisy tried to lift her head. The shafts of pain she experienced as a result persuaded her to lie still again.

Reuben stood up, and Daisy saw him pour water from a small jug into a beaker and bring it to her. 'Can you take a few sips of this, my dear?'

His arm slid below her shoulders and eased her slowly up from the pillows till she could sip a little from the beaker.

'Please ask the doctor to come,' Reuben said to the lady.

'I'll leave the door open, Reuben,' she said before doing as he asked. Daisy heard her feet patter across the landing and the slither of her skirts as she descended.

'Where am I?' she asked. 'Where is ...' She paused, wondering what the word just out of reach might be. 'Smithers? Do I usually have Smithers with me?'

'Do you remember anything else?' Reuben asked.

'Yes,' Daisy said. 'I remember that none of my family answers my questions with any honesty.'

'Ah!' She watched Reuben retreat from her side and set the water on a table. 'I'm afraid that isn't going to change much over the next few days, my dear.'

'Mr Bazkeley,' a man said as he bustled into the room. 'I see your niece has come round.'

Daisy looked at Reuben. Her uncle? She thought perhaps she had uncles and they might be Spanish. She did not believe Reuben was one such, however.

'Now then, little lady,' the man said, and Daisy decided to dislike him intensely, but only after he had restored her to her feet.

'I'll wait downstairs, sir,' Reuben said, and disappeared.

Daisy sighed. She had a strong feeling she ought to be somewhere else. She had a strong feeling all was not as the doctor believed. She knew Reuben was behind the mischief, whatever the mischief was.

13

London, 1828

Mrs John Brent stepped onto the short stair in front of her London house. A small boy wriggled in her arms, and behind her another stood beside his papa, gazing curiously around.

'Papa, why are the houses so close together in London town?' the lad piped, and the watcher smiled.

Mrs Brent glanced down to ensure her feet found the steps safely, and when she lifted her head, recognition made her exclaim, 'Daisy!'

The small boys reacted to the urgency in their mama's voice and set an uproar in train. A nursemaid took the baby from Mrs Brent, and a footman distracted the older boy while his parents moved forward as one.

'How d'ye do, Lady Daisy,' John said stiffly, and Daisy stifled a laugh. It would not do to tread on his sensibilities so soon after he had agreed to this meeting. The days of teasing him and poking fun at his old-fashioned views were long gone.

Elspeth Brent, on the other hand, rushed down the front steps and threw herself onto her cousin. Daisy was crushed by the strength of her embrace.

'Daisy, I have missed you so very much, and I am pleased that you are spending time in London while we are here, too.' Elspeth linked her arm through Daisy's, and with a quick glance behind to see that John and the boys with their attendants were following, set them off towards Hyde Park. 'Where is the redoubtable Smithers?'

'Waiting in the carriage. You and John are all the escort I need. You look so well, Elspeth. Marriage and motherhood clearly suit you beyond anything.'

'Certainly beyond looking after cantankerous old women,' Elspeth replied briskly, but she did not refer to either of her parents; and Daisy, in deference to her understandable feelings on that subject, remained silent. 'And you, cousin, you are also looking well.'

'Thank you, my dear. I have been up in town most Seasons since the disastrous one in 'twenty-two,' Daisy said, then wished the ground would swallow her. She had rehearsed what she might say to Elspeth so often, but it had all gone from her head on seeing her cousin look so charming and happy.

'Do not look so conscious, Daisy. I have winkled most of the story out of John over the years, and I know he has returned some of your letters to me unopened. I have to thank you for persevering in the face of his obduracy.' Elspeth increased her pace. Daisy realised she was forcing John to decide whether to stay with his children or speed up and join them. A gap appeared between the two parts of their party.

'John was undoubtedly very hurt by the events around the time of Toby and Mariah's marriage,' Daisy said equably. She still experienced a sour rise of bilious discomfort when she thought of the disdain with which he had treated her explanations. However, he had married her cousin very soon after, and as their own betrothal had not been published beyond the family, no others were any the wiser.

'That remark is generous beyond any expectation the goose deserves,' Elspeth exclaimed. 'He was simply wrong to discount Reuben Longreach's actions for your safety, and the earl was wrong to exile *him* from the family.'

Daisy tugged the lace of her summer gloves and twitched the strings of her reticule. There were one or two truths she could not yet share with Elspeth, much as she had always valued her older cousin's good sense. That night, all those years ago, Reuben had acted without consulting any of the other men, and destroyed her betrothal irrevocably. Although there had always been a lady with them when she lay in a strange bed, lapsing in and out of consciousness, John had refused to accept it.

'*I have found you and Reuben in several compromising events*,' Toby had said when she was eventually restored to Grosvenor Square, three days after the wedding. *'How can I insist John honour his promises when you are unable to tell us what happened?'*

How indeed? Daisy had tried so hard to recall what had caused her loss of memory and the scar on her head, but it was no use. The best doctors Toby could find were only able to say she might remember one day. In the meantime, her mama should keep a close eye on *all other matters*.

She was sure Reuben had acted with the utmost propriety, and there were no *other matters* to destroy her young life. Even without any, her reputation would have suffered abominably had they not been able to give out that she had taken ill with fever and spots, so her immediate removal from the wedding celebrations was essential.

Only now, six years later, John Brent still smarted. Daisy had decided the moment had come to push for some effective contact with her lovely Scottish cousin and the little boys her mama would love to dote on nearly as much as her grandchildren from Toby and Mariah. Daisy was so glad to finally meet them, and she would bring John round. He joined them and watched the footman race off after the older boy and a ball.

'Jasper runs well, do you not think, Lady Daisy?'

'John, please,' Elspeth pleaded. 'We agreed you would try to welcome Daisy.'

'John, it grieves me to know you are still hurt, and I would have it any other way, but I cannot turn back the clock.' Daisy smiled at her cousin and her former betrothed. 'Seeing you so very happy with Elspeth makes me understand we might not have been suited.'

'We might not?' John asked, and it was almost a squeak.

'No, we might not. I am convinced we were drawn together by our mutual love of Toby and by the difficulties my inheritance strewed between us, which I regarded as an unusually attractive challenge.'

'Indeed, you were most assertive over that issue.' John looked thoughtful, and Daisy pressed home her advantage.

'I knew you would see the matter clearly once time had intervened to dampen the coals of your anxiety.'

'There was much anxiety. That bounder Longreach took too much on himself,' John said. Daisy heard the curiosity creeping into his tone, and her spirits lifted further. How John must have longed for the true story all these years. Gossip was one of his main interests in life.

'Of course, if my uncle had succeeded with his plan of removing Elspeth from the house, then matters would have been very different.'

'But Papa was thwarted, and we must continue to give thanks for that,' Elspeth intervened. Daisy remembered how often her quiet common sense had saved them all when arguments threatened.

Daisy watched little Jasper kick his ball into a shrub and scramble on all fours in behind it. Soon enough, they heard his childish shouts: 'Papa, Papa, come into my tunnel. It's a deep tunnel like your coal ones. Do come here, Papa.'

The ladies watched as John dropped to all fours and peered into Jasper's tunnel. Soon he was deep in discussion with the child, and they could speak more freely again.

'Elspeth, I would see you alone, if you are able to secure some time to make a visit, please?' Daisy asked.

* * *

Reuben Longreach gazed at the front of his cousin's townhouse in Grosvenor Square. The days when he might bound up the steps and expect Stephens to admit him whether the earl was in residence or not were long gone, and he sighed. Daisy had cost them all dearly by her night-time wanderings and sheer devilment. He had received a summons from the earl, however, and he came.

'Mr Longreach, sir. I am pleased to see you back here in the family home,'

Stephens said as he took Reuben's hat, gloves and stick.

'Thank you, Stephens. It is good to see you continue in harness.'

'His lordship likes me to oversee things, sir, although young Matt and that scamp, Josh, are the ones who do late nights now. Come this way, sir; the earl is waiting for you.'

Inside Toby's study, the two men executed tidy, polite bows and few words while Stephens hovered. Once the elderly butler had closed the door on them, however, they embraced warmly.

'Four months, Reuben, since our dinner in White's. It's too long, man. Did you arrive in the Low Countries in time to see their canals frozen?'

'I did, and to hear some good music. Is your brandy still as good as my memory tells?'

'Judge for yourself,' Toby said, pouring large measures. They settled into comfortable chairs and studied each other in silence for a few moments.

'How are the ladies?' Reuben asked at

last. 'The baby's spots were causing Lady Mellon a lot of heartache, if I remember.'

'The ladies are all well, Reuben. The baby walks on unsteady feet, and Mariah may be increasing again. Her papa's death was a huge sadness, as you may imagine.' Toby's gaze clouded and Reuben acknowledged the news. He knew how much Toby had enjoyed the older man's company.

'I am sorry to hear of that. The household will be diminished. Does the dowager continue in good health?'

'Robust,' Toby said with such strength of feeling that Reuben wondered if he had been summoned in relation to her affairs. 'Robust, and fretting about Daisy's single state. She is … '

'Twenty-four next Tuesday,' Reuben said, completing his cousin's speech. 'She has grown into her looks.'

'When did you see her?' Although Toby asked, Reuben knew he would not be very surprised. London society was small enough still that their paths had to cross occasionally.

'I spotted your party last week when I took my seat at Evan's recital. Obviously, I left at the interval in order to avoid causing her any embarrassment.'

'Did you?' Toby clipped. 'Tell me, Reuben — and please do nothing to spare Daisy's embarrassment — why did it take her so long to recover her memory?'

'Doctors have given you many opinions on that matter, sir. Surely you cannot believe I have any greater knowledge.' Reuben set his glass on a side table with a decided snap of irritation. They had been over this ground on several occasions, and Toby had sensibly ignored the holes in Daisy's arguments.

'Please, Reuben, do not lie to me any longer. My mama is close to driving me into nervous exhaustion. Mariah is likewise beset by instruction and counter-instruction over hosting events and finding eligible men who might have the backbone to marry her redoubtable sister-in-law.' Toby stood and paced the carpet. 'I will ask again: who was she?'

Reuben knew the game was over as far

as his past association was concerned. He would be able to rely on Toby's discretion, but he regretted the need to make the name public nonetheless.

'Lady Phoebe Sandison.'

'Lady Phoebe,' Toby mused. 'Her husband died in a fishing accident, I think.'

'He did. Our association started three years after Phoebe was widowed, and did not survive Daisy's injury.'

'I see,' Toby said, and Reuben heard the import of his words sinking into his cousin's understanding. 'So the lady who accompanied Daisy at all times through those days was your mistress?'

'An ugly word, I think; but yes, she was.' Reuben shifted his weight and stretched his long legs in front. 'You will understand I was not *keeping* Phoebe. Sandison left her properly provided for with a jointure and a house in London, as well as the slightly musty keep in Strath Halladale.'

'Did he?' Toby speared his dark brown gaze at Reuben and he flinched. 'Why did you not think to tell me, or Mr Brent, in whose house you had secreted his betrothed? A respectable small inn was a description we both found a little hard to accept.'

'I gave Phoebe my word that if she received us, no one would be told. I'm breaking it now because I imagine you have already worked out most of the remaining parts of the story.'

'Oh yes.' The earl nodded. 'Curiously, it was Daisy who provided the final clue. Lady Sandison and her sons were at a card party we attended, and when Mama afterwards commented on the fine silk Lady Sandison wore, Daisy said she'd always had excellent taste. Anyone interested would puzzle over how she knew what Lady Sandison's taste might be, as we had never been known to be in close company with her before.'

'She wore Lady Sandison's clothes until Smithers sent a bag of her own to my lodgings.' Reuben smiled at the memory. 'The dresses were a little short in the ankle, but in the circumstances . . . '

'As you say.' The earl stopped pacing, and Reuben felt the intensity of his stare.

'We are now six years into my marriage; Mariah has presented me with healthy issue. All should be well.'

'Toby, you are not ill, are you?' Reuben searched the earl's face for signs of suffering etched by pain, but although Toby had been growing greyer around the temples, there was no marked change in his appearance.

'Yes, I am ill. I am ill with worry over what ridiculous idea my mama and her companion will dredge up next. Daisy must be married.'

Reuben drew an unsteady breath. While he had every intention that Daisy be married, it did not suit him to have the earl dictating any sort of timetable. 'You cannot be blind to the opposition she would set up if you chose a man of whom she did not approve,' he said crisply.

'No, I am fully aware of the ingenuity she employs to defeat both my mama's and my own efforts to see her respectably settled,' Toby agreed. 'It is almost as if she had her heart settled elsewhere.'

Reuben drank a fair measure of brandy

before daring to add anything to this. The earl might be exasperated, but he was not stupid. Instead, Reuben chose to steer their talk away from this potentially dangerous conversation. 'I appeared to be in that position, too, in respect of Miss Howie — Mrs Brent, as she is now. Although, of course, my attentions to her were only in pursuit of our plans to frustrate the abduction and ransom demand. I still find myself amazed that Lady Beatrice was fooled by Pemmican's promises over the breaking of the trust.'

Reuben had willingly gone up to Edinburgh when asked, and it was his word that set in motion the early investigations over the activities of Lady Beatrice. It was he who had said to Toby, 'The neighbour I spoke to in Queen Street, a Mistress Jemma Baker, has seen many items removed from the house during the night. She is a young woman with several small children at her feet. I think she wakes in the dark hours and goes to them when the nanny is overwhelmed.'

The one thing they were all convinced of was the immutable nature of the provisions of the last will and testament governing the family trust. The assets of the trust could not be sold off without extended court action. So Pemmican had fooled Lady Beatrice into believing she could achieve the impossible, if only she kept paying him to keep presenting it to the courts.

'Poor Elspeth.' The earl toyed a little with his brandy glass. 'You know, Reuben, I have wondered whether Aunt Beatrice's behaviour was more to do with protecting Elspeth. Howie was a desperate man, and that harridan of a mother had an iron grip over the whole family.'

Reuben had to still his tongue. Deep dislike of Lady Beatrice could hardly be swept away in an instant, but he began to understand what Toby was hinting at. 'You think perhaps she feared for Elspeth's safety and saw Pemmican's proposals to get capital from the trust as a lesser evil?'

'Possibly. I cannot believe she wanted

Elspeth cast onto the mercies of a pack of sailors. I think that though she may not have known of those plans, she suspected her husband and mama-in-law were plotting something along those lines.'

It had been a horrible time for the whole family, and they might never have exposed the plot to kidnap Elspeth if Farquerson had not sent a letter from the *Leith Rose* by a messenger. His captain had been drinking with associates who were preparing a ship to receive a lady connected with the nobility — a lady whose wealthy cousin would pay to have her restored. The wealthy cousin would not, they thought, kick up too much of a fuss, because he'd so recently escaped a murder charge.

'How does Lady Beatrice go on?' Reuben enquired, hoping to get a little time to adjust his opinion of her. 'There was a ploy afoot to move her further north, I think?'

'My mama corresponds with her, but refuses to meet her. She is housed in Berwick with a small staff. Howie's entire property was forfeited when the banks called in, so she has no house to call her own.' Toby sighed, and Reuben kept quiet, watching his expression fluctuate. It was a measure of the man that he'd continued to keep command of his household while history threatened to repeat itself within two weeks.

'Ah well, we prevailed, Reuben — and no small thanks to the ship's mate you made such a good impression on. Now, to my sister.' Toby made a deprecatory movement of his hand, and Reuben held his breath. 'I am no magician, and I realise I must have help in seeing her settled. If Mariah and I are to enjoy any kind of normal life, then she must be married and removed from my roof. Daisy continues to be in awe of the countess — and that is no bad thing, for she has been unruly in the past; but Mariah finds a barrier of sorts when she tries to engage Daisy in talk about her future. It seems she is held back by something.'

Reuben wondered if Toby could be right — had Daisy's heart settled elsewhere? He did hope so.

'I think,' the earl was talking again, and Reuben brought his attention to bear, 'the moment has come for you to be received here openly once more.'

'Thank you, Toby. I have missed my visits to the house.'

'And I know the house has missed you. At least the musical instruments have. It will be a delight to hear them played again, properly.' Reuben watched his cousin fiddle with some papers on the huge mahogany desk that dominated the room. 'You are the only person I can trust to assist with Daisy's future. There are presently two young men in contention. One is Norman, Lord Stanhold's heir, and the other is Mr Archibald Campbell. I am minded to favour the suit of Archibald Campbell of Argyll.'

'Archie Campbell? He has very red hair.'

'What? Reuben, do not make frivolous remarks, please. He is a scion of the ducal family, although not so close that Daisy would ever become a duchess.'

Toby stopped fiddling and cast Reuben a serious look. 'Make no mistake, I will have Daisy married and out of my house. Dearly as I love her, I love my wife more.'

Reuben wondered whether Toby thought his actual presence would afflict Daisy enough to drive her into the arms of a Norman Stanhold or an Archie Campbell. Well, no matter. It suited him very well to be there in order to make quite sure Daisy made no further wrong choices.

14

Daisy turned over in her bed and sat up abruptly.

'Reuben!' She breathed the word onto the night-dark air, then pushed aside the bedding and tipped her weight over the edge. This was another hopeless dream of his return, and she was cross with herself for believing it again.

Only, there was music. Haunting melodies hung suspended in her memory, and she could not quite convince herself it was a trick played by an exhausted brain. Her head played fewer tricks in recent months, but since she'd begun to notice Reuben among the summer visitors at concerts, and across the park or the crowded shopping streets, vivid dreams had come again.

There were real sightings, too. Why else would her mama discover a sudden wish to retire to the carriage, or Mariah ask her to hold little Connie while she did something? Yes, Reuben Longreach, distant cousin — seven removes separated him now from the earldom since young Fred's arrival — and charlatan, was openly back in Town.

But that did not mean he was back in Grosvenor Square. Toby knew how his very name afflicted her. He knew how she grew short of breath and pink in the face when Reuben's name was necessarily mentioned in connection with the scandalous behaviour of their aunt. Fortunately, he did not know that it was Lady Phoebe Sandison's association with Reuben that caused Daisy the greatest pain.

She hauled her wrapper over her night things and pushed her feet into the embroidered slippers Archie Campbell's sister had pressed on her as a gift only last week. Mr Campbell had been travelling in the east and had come home with all manner of exotic items. His sister had distributed them among her friends and had tapped Daisy's arm lightly when she handed them over. 'I do not say Archie wishes to see you wear them, but he particularly asked that I should save this pair for you,' Susan had said confidentially. 'He is very admiring of a woman who does so much for a cause.'

The slippers were enchantingly embroidered with two cranes wrapped around each other in conjugal bliss. Daisy dared not think too deeply about the significance of Miss Campbell's words, lest she be obliged to send them back.

She was left to wonder whether the cause Mr Campbell so admired was the Foundling Hospital or the Archie Campbell exotic travelling fund. Like so many of the young men who paid court to her, he had boundless confidence in his lineage and its power to hide his lack of funds. On the other hand, she had to marry someone, and he was very diverting.

Daisy opened the door of her bedroom and stopped to listen. If anyone was playing the pianoforte, they were in the library on the ground floor. She heard the muffled footsteps of the night watchman leave his post by the door and move towards the kitchen passage. Light from his candle flickered around the walls and disappeared as he moved off. The big door into the servants' quarters slid closed with a sigh on its huge hinges, and darkness crept back. Except there was a line of light …

Goose-bumps dotted Daisy's skin. Only Reuben played in that manner. The music flowed along her nerves, tingling like springwater in its freshness. Would she go down? How could she not?

With the confidence of many such descents, Daisy counted her way along the landing to the banister and then down the curving central staircase. She dropped onto the tiles and paused. How could it be Reuben, practising in a house where he was not welcome, and in fact banned?

She floated across the wide expanse of hall and wondered why the night man had gone off his post. He would hardly have deserted the hall when an intruder was using the pianoforte, so either he knew the player or knew that the player was welcomed by the earl. Connie's music master did not come visiting at midnight.

While the great clocks and the little ones chimed in the new day, Daisy pushed open the door of the library. Sitting on the pianoforte's velvet-covered bench, wearing a dark-coloured banyan over his shirt and evening trousers, was the man who inhabited her dreams.

'Reuben.'

'Daisy.'

Later, she remembered how her eyes had drunk in every detail of his appearance. The strong length of him sat very still, allowing her scrutiny, maybe enjoying its intensity, because she detected the upwards curve of a questioning eyebrow. His hair was still dark and unruly, but he had it caught at the nape in a thin ribbon so it did not escape and tickle his face while he concentrated on the music.

She let her eyes linger a little on the planes of his face, darkened by his night beard at this time of day, and then dropped her gaze to the loose material of his shirt. The linen gaped across his chest, and she closed her eyes abruptly when she realised curls of dark hair peeped through the neck opening.

Reuben's feet were bare, and she drew a sharp little breath at their vulnerable appearance on the uncarpeted floor beneath the pianoforte. He hooked some leather slippers out of hiding and shucked them on before standing up and bowing.

'Good evening, Lady Daisy. I trust my playing was not responsible for disturbing you. The night man may not have closed the door properly after he left me here.'

'You were playing for the watchman?' she asked, and immediately realised what a stupid remark it must sound to him.

'No. I was playing for myself. I give a recital on Friday, and alas my practising is a little behind schedule,' he said, and she felt heat spiral through her as it so often had when Reuben spoke only to her. The power of her own speech deserted her.

She had dreamt this so often that even now she was unsure whether the Reuben in front of her was a figment of her imaginings or a man of flesh and blood. She crossed the room and set a hand on the pianoforte. It was solid, and the wood of its casing felt cool and polished.

Reuben moved gracefully towards her and slid a hand around her waist, lowering her onto the velvet-covered bench. His smell teased memories, and she shrank from the intimacy of his touch.

'How dare you touch me?' she whispered into the silence. 'How dare you come back and haunt me?'

'I thought you might faint, my dear ...'

'I am not your dear.' Daisy gritted the words from a well of loathing that surprised even herself. She would have risen, but suspected her legs would not hold her upright, so great was the shock of seeing him again at such close quarters.

Reuben sat down, and drawing her close, covered her lips in a blistering kiss. He felt the thundering beat of her heart as it struggled to keep her conscious. Her limbs were limp. The half-remembered smells of lemon and lavender invaded his senses.

Her mouth eased open beneath the urgent pressure of his lips, and he tempted fate a little by stroking the muscles of her back. When she stirred, he brought both hands to clasp the sides of her face and hold her head steady.

Daisy slid an arm around his neck and her sleeve fell away. He glanced at the arm and thought she was slimmer than he remembered or liked. He stood up, bringing her with him, reluctantly breaking the kiss. With one smooth movement he lifted her into his arms and crossed the library.

It was dark in the hall, where only a hooded lantern burned beside the watchman's chair. He had not returned from the kitchens, and Reuben moved rapidly onto the staircase. Daisy turned her head into the hollow of his shoulder and let her arm slide onto his back. Her night-robe threatened to slide out of its ties, and he tucked the material beneath her thighs as he powered up the main stairs towards her room.

The door was ajar and he shouldered it open. He kicked it shut behind them and slowed down. There was hardly any light. The logs of a late fire glowed when the draught from the door fanned them. It allowed Reuben to orientate himself and cross to the bed. He set Daisy onto the rumpled sheets.

'I trust, sir, you will be leaving now,' Daisy said.

'Will you scream for help?' he teased, knowing full and well Daisy needed help from no one.

'Why, yes. What else does a well-bred daughter do in such circumstances?'

He was pleased to hear the spark of defiance that had so characterised the old Daisy, and laughed. 'The drawl you used to scare John Brent, my dear, doesn't move me. Besides, it would certainly prompt me to kiss you again and secure your silence.' He moved away from the bed. He needed to calm his racing pulse, and breathing in Daisy's scent was not the way to do that.

'What are you about, Reuben Longreach? Why have you come back?'

'I haven't ever been very far away.' Reuben eased across the floor until he found a chair by backing his calves against it, and sank down. 'And Toby has always had my direction.'

'Toby —'

'Toby,' Reuben interrupted. 'I cannot tell for certain how the earl views your faradiddle of lies, half-lies, and wishful thinking over your lost nights surrounding his wedding, but I believe him to be a man of superior intelligence.'

'I told no lies,' she protested. He watched her movements become more agitated, but he could not make out her expression. The room was too dark now the logs had died entirely.

'Don't you have a candle on your night-stand?' he asked, and waited while she struck a light. A yellow glow lit her face from below, and Reuben caught his breath.

When he had been forced to retreat six

years ago, Daisy was on the verge of womanhood. She had grown into that early promise of great beauty. The Longreach height and symmetrical features were complemented by olive-toned skin from her mama's Spanish heritage. He had seen her from a distance in crowds and across badly lit rooms, but now, in the intimacy of candlelight, he saw how very beautiful she was.

'I told no lies,' she repeated more forcefully.

'I did not hear your explanations, and Toby did not repeat all his conversations with you, but I think you omitted to mention that Lady Phoebe Sandison had mopped up your wound,' Reuben said.

'Why would I mention the lady's name? How would I explain the familiarity you enjoyed with her, and the easy access you had to her house?' Daisy sat ramrod-straight and very still.

'Don't you want to say, 'and her bed'? I did attempt to tell you that final afternoon that I had been with a lady, but you would not allow it because you were so focused on marrying me off to your cousin.'

'If we are to accuse one another of lying, then that is the biggest yet. You were at the docks, Reuben Longreach. You tried to dissuade me from asking questions by telling me about *a lady* in such a manner that I could not believe it.'

'So when I told you the truth, your conclusion was that I lied; and when the truth was presented to you in person, your decision was to conceal it,' Reuben pursued her arguments relentlessly. 'Why did you not tell Toby that Lady Phoebe was my mistress?'

'Get out.'

'As you wish, but you should expect to see a lot more of me than a fleeting glimpse across concert halls, Daisy. Toby has invited me to make an extended visit.'

He left Daisy's room silently and listened for the watchman's footsteps, but there was nothing. He crossed the landing and would have turned towards the bachelors' quarters when his eye was caught by a discarded slipper.

'Mnm,' he murmured as he held the embroidered frippery in his hand. 'I wonder how this can be used to good effect?' He tucked it into the pocket of his banyan.

* * *

Daisy sat as calmly as she could manage while Smithers dressed her hair. She had taken a breakfast tray instead of descending to confront Toby, Mariah, and Reuben in the breakfast room, and now she proposed to go out without meeting them either. It was cowardly and useless as a strategy, she knew, but her behaviour the previous night had rattled her confidence.

She'd sat on in the soft glow of her candle until she was certain Reuben would not return, brushing tears impatiently from her cheeks. This could not be happening, she'd thought.

But it was. Reuben Longreach was back in her home; and her brother, who had so recently welcomed Norman

Stanhold and Mr Archibald Campbell and his sister into their circle of friends, was assisting in his rehabilitation as if nothing untoward had happened.

Daisy threw off her wrapper and rolled into the bedclothes. Reuben had kissed her, and she had lain in his arms as though hit by a lightning strike. Why had she gone to him as if she were going to a returning husband?

Now in the late-morning light, there were other problems to face.

'I looked very carefully along the landing, my lady, and so far as the library door. Mr Longreach was in there whistling one of his tunes, and when he caught sight of me, he asked if he could help me with anything,' Smithers said, and sniffed. 'If you were to ask me, your ladyship, he knew what I wanted. He raised one of his eyebrows in that way he has.'

'Why would he take one of my slippers?' Daisy mused, and mistress and maid exchanged glances through the mirror. 'I suppose it was him, and not one of the children? Connie is very fond of the cranes.'

'I don't think Nanny has brought the children down this morning, my lady, but I will ask. Discreetly, of course.'

Daisy rose and settled a short cape around her shoulders. She took her gloves and parasol from Smithers and set off for the front door, where she expected to find the town carriage waiting for her expedition.

Reuben stood in the hall. She wondered if his complexion had always been quite so high. Surely the sight of her in her new season's pink silk taffeta morning dress could not be responsible for the sudden flush that suffused his features.

'Good morning, Daisy,' he said. He crossed to the foot of the stairs and extended a hand to assist her descent. 'Toby and Mariah were disappointed you did not come in to breakfast, as they wanted to help ease our first meeting after so many years.'

'After so many years,' she repeated. This was clever, of course, because it wouldn't be quite the thing to let the household know they had met in the dark hours, when she was dressed for bed, Daisy thought. 'I had not expected to see you here, cousin.'

'As to the relationship between us, I wonder if we might meet simply as friends. The cousinship is of such distance that I do not dwell on it in society,' Reuben said with an edge to his voice that piqued her interest.

'And yet, why are you here making free of the earl's house if you do not rely on our relationship?' It was shrewish and she knew it, but could not prevent the words escaping. Reuben's presence was going to turn the house into a kind of gilded prison.

'Daisy,' came Mariah's voice, a little sharply. 'What are you thinking of? Toby has invited Reuben to make an extended visit while he is presenting a series of concerts to benefit the Foundling Hospital. He had hoped to make this known to you at breakfast, but you were a lie-a-bed today.'

'Good morning, Mariah. I didn't see you arrive. Yes, I did not sleep very well, and I thought I would take a tray instead of coming down,' Daisy replied. She twiddled the point of her parasol around on the tiles and studied it intently. To look at Reuben again might have been her undoing.

'I'm sorry to hear that, my dear.' Mariah was instantly full of sisterly concern, and Daisy experienced a pang of remorse. Mariah had always shown kindness and understanding over Daisy's missing days. The more commendable, as they had prevented Toby and her from leaving for the country and a honeymoon of tranquillity such as they had expected to enjoy.

'A brisk walk will help to clear my head. I am meeting Miss Campbell,' Daisy said, and would have moved around them, but Reuben stopped her.

'May I join you? I spent some hours practising last night, and a brisk walk would also benefit me. Besides, I have heard much about Miss Campbell and her explorer brother. I would like to make her acquaintance.'

'If you must,' Daisy replied with no grace. She heard her sister-in-law's sharp intake of breath but could make no effort to reassure her. Reuben was about his tricks again, and Daisy was clearly the target. 'Smithers will join us.'

15

Daisy saw Susan Campbell and Archie as soon as she descended from the town carriage. They waited beside a small plantation of colourful shrubs, and Mr Campbell had obviously been examining them.

'I see Mr Campbell does not worry about mud stains,' Reuben murmured in her ear as he took her arm in a firm grip and set off towards the Scottish couple. 'But I knew that of old. He occasionally appeared in White's before his latest expedition, and often, as now, had twigs of interesting foliage sticking out of his pockets.'

Daisy found the urge to laugh all but overpowering. How did Reuben achieve this, when for several weeks now she had been enamoured of Mr Campbell's stories and adventures in the furthest reaches of their known world? 'Within seconds, you try to make me see schoolboy knees and puppyish enthusiasm. Does it not occur to you, sir, that Mr Campbell simply disdains stuffy convention and erudite opinion?'

'You know, I played for you last night, my dear,' Reuben said, ignoring her outburst. It was barely above a whisper, but the words caught Daisy's ear and set up a yearning in her soul. 'I wanted our first meeting to be a private one so you could shout, or faint, without any interested family audience.'

Daisy brought her head round sharply and caught the expression of deep understanding in his clever eyes. How could he wrong-foot her so easily? she puzzled.

Before she could make any response, the Campbells were upon them. 'Good morning, Lady Daisy,' they chorused, and waited politely for introductions to be made.

While the others were exchanging bows, Daisy cast a quizzical look towards Smithers and followed the line of her maid's glance to where a tall man in unkempt dark clothing slid back into the protection of an overhanging tree. His outline was familiar. It made her stomach muscles clench in anxiety. Had he been watching the Campbells? she wondered.

As she turned back to the group, she saw how Reuben's shoulders had stiffened. He had seen and recognised the man, she felt sure, and when he turned his deep gaze back to her she knew without doubt. But who was he?

They agreed to walk around the Serpentine pond. Reuben easily manoeuvred the group so that Daisy and Susan walked ahead and he was beside Archie. Daisy imagined him shortening his stride to avoid forcing the ladies to hurry, and remembered another walk when John Brent was injured and Elspeth helped them all keep up a pace he could deal with.

Did I wonder even then whether Reuben was the one man who could match me?

The words set off a panic in her head, and she hoped Miss Campbell would attribute the sudden flare of heat to her brother's presence. 'How did you spend yesterday evening, Miss Campbell?' she asked. 'Is your mama recovering from her indisposition?'

Daisy deliberately pulled her thoughts back to the present and the necessity of finding an acceptable husband. Toby and Mariah had been very kind, but she could not trespass on their good nature forever.

I cannot marry Reuben. Lady Phoebe will be forever between us.

'Mama is a little brighter this morning, thank you. She sadly suffers every year when the roses bloom in profusion. In fact, I wonder if it does not begin when the trees come into leaf,' Susan said thoughtfully. Daisy knew the girl was interested in the work her brother did, and could explain more clearly many of the things he tried to explain. She had a dry wit, too, which endeared her to Mariah.

'Really? Does this mean she has to spend much of the summer indoors?' Daisy knew she allowed a touch of dismay to enter her tone, but she could not imagine passing an entire summer inside.

'That would be wise, but she will come out and follow Archie around as he monitors his specimens. Argyll is fertile ground for bringing on the small plants and tree seeds he brings back. Already we are achieving success with the ones from his trip two years ago.' The girl's voice was brimming with pride, and Daisy wondered if her own ever would. Flowers were cut and left in the garden room for her to arrange. Fruit came from the hothouses in Hampshire. Vegetables came from ... She could hardly remember if she knew where they came from.

I really cannot marry Archie Campbell unless I discover a little more enthusiasm for the mundane elements of his science.

She lost the rhythm of her steps as the knowledge hit her. Archie Campbell was a lovely man. His sister was adoring and adorable. But were they people Daisy could spend the rest of her life with? Would it be even more dishonest than a marriage to John Brent?

'Daisy, Toby has suggested the

Grosvenor Square house might be used for an exclusive recital to raise money for an educational cause,' Reuben spoke from behind them, and she and Susan slowed to allow the men to catch them up. 'He is minded to show the countess his love and thanks for the delivery of young Frederick.'

'Why, that is a very romantic notion, sir,' Susan said brightly. 'Archie and I attended one of your recitals three years ago in Hanover Square. We enjoyed it immensely.' She smiled shyly.

'Did you, Miss Campbell? I am glad. Mr Campbell, do you have another expedition planned?' Reuben asked briskly, and Daisy picked up on his thoughts as if the intervening six years had washed away. He was going to offer to raise money for Archie Campbell and get him out of their orbit. She fumed. It was one thing for her to wonder whether she could marry Mr Campbell, but Reuben had no business to make interference in her betrothal plans — just as he had done six years ago.

'Are you thinking that an expedition

might be funded?' she asked before Archie Campbell could reply. 'Mr Campbell has only recently returned from an extended trip, and might have other matters in his life to attend to.'

'I see your disturbed night has not affected your faculties, my dear. Were we to suggest Mr Campbell's cause to your sister, I'm sure she would be most interested.' Reuben sent her a glance full of challenging fire.

Archie Campbell's complexion flared and paled for several changes before he was able to think of a reply. 'Mr Longreach, this is beyond anything I might have dreamed of ...' He stuttered to a halt and Daisy waited impatiently, but there was nothing else.

She saw Susan blench when Archie's gaze swung round towards the place they had last seen the tall man, and suddenly she remembered who he was. Mr Albert Pemmican had been Lady Beatrice's lawyer. He'd turned up at the house shortly after she was restored to her family, and implied things that were too awful to contemplate. Although Daisy had not been a party to the discussion between him and the earl, she'd gleaned enough from Smithers and the servants' grapevine to make her heart feel as if it were breaking.

She stared at Reuben in horror. Why had the lawyer turned up again as soon as he was back in residence in Grosvenor Square? Not for a single moment had it crossed her mind that Reuben could have been involved in assisting her aunt and uncle — and yet now, Pemmican had reappeared. She tried to remind herself that Reuben had not known of her plans to join Mr Campbell and Susan here this morning. It must surely be a coincidence.

But Daisy did not believe in coincidences. Reuben already knew *of* Mr Campbell. He'd said as much. What if he actually *knew* Mr Campbell? She felt the rising rush of questions begin to overwhelm her as they did whenever she was at her desk writing her fictions. The morning was losing its bloom.

Had Reuben, in fact, acted as a go-between for Aunt Beatrice and Pemmican, while also acting as a double agent by doing Toby's errands, too?

Bile rose in her throat. She could not shake the sense of how these things all came together. She longed to be safely back in Grosvenor Square with Toby and Mariah.

* * *

'Your departure was abrupt enough to leave your friends wondering how they had insulted you,' Reuben charged when he cornered Daisy in the garden room later that day. Her wish to interview the earl and question him about the number of coincidences related to Reuben and Mr Albert Pemmican had been frustrated. Toby, Mariah and the two infants had gone calling on John Brent and Elspeth.

'I am unable to help that,' she said, and turned her shoulder on him. He was intuitive enough to work out what was in fact troubling her, and she was no longer sure if she could dissemble. She raised a rose stem and measured the length with a practised eye.

'I saw Pemmican, as you did, this morning,' he said. 'How did you recognise him?'

Her secateurs were poised to trim the stem, but at his words she cut it in half. 'He came to the house after you brought me home, six years ago. I was not, of course, allowed to join the discussions, but Toby told me about some of them later. It seems he was helping Aunt Beatrice attempt to change the terms of the family trust.'

'He was,' Reuben agreed. 'Toby has said how keen he was to stress that this was the full extent of Lady Beatrice's involvement, and that they knew nothing of the kidnapping plot.'

Daisy heard uncertainty in Reuben's voice, as if he was weighing up his words. They all knew how wicked Aunt Beatrice had been.

'He had the impertinence to offer me his card once, in case I ever had need of rescuing from a young man's troubles.' Reuben spoke quietly, but she was not fooled. He was tempting her into divulging the troublesome thoughts she would only discuss with Toby.

'You've been meeting Toby over the years, Reuben, and I know he will have explained this to you.' She snipped another flower and set it into the scrunched-up bundle of wire in a large china bowl.

'The hopeless plan to upset the trust,' Reuben mused. 'Pemmican knew it would take a lifetime or longer, but he expected to fool them. They'd already used many of your aunt's inherited valuables to keep paying him and hold the creditors at bay.'

'Yes, Toby told me of your conversation with Aunt Beatrice's neighbour — Mistress Baker, was it? I suppose we must assume that was why Elspeth was kept upstairs in the Edinburgh house, as she could not hear the discussions or interfere when another item was removed.' Daisy shook her head. She worked on the flowers silently while she thought over her older cousin's restricted life.

'Howie, of course, knew the trust would not be changed soon enough to help him clear his debts.' Reuben lifted a short branch of greenery and, leaning around Daisy, added it to her arrangement. She tweaked it and the whole thing fell apart.

'Now I must begin again,' she protested. 'What are you doing in here, Reuben?'

'Talking to you. Is it not one of your frustrations that we males do not keep you properly informed?'

'Or properly hoodwinked,' she said bluntly.

'Uncharitable, my dear,' Reuben spoke softly, and how she wished she could believe him, but the coincidences mounted up in her thoughts. 'Howie decided to have Elspeth kidnapped and held to ransom. I encountered him and Pemmican in the company of his coachman, who was armed with a cudgel. Though it made me wonder about my personal safety, I did not think Howie would subject his daughter to the sort of thing it turned out they had planned. Your sortie into the lane that night was a complication we did not want or need.'

'No. I can understand that I would have achieved a much higher ransom than Elspeth, being Toby's sister rather than a mere cousin.'

'You would,' Reuben said, with matter-of-fact unconcern for her sensibilities.

'Perhaps if I had been allowed to know what was happening, I would not have tried to kick over the traces,' she said. She set the final flowers among her reinstated foliage and stepped back — against Reuben's chest. When had he moved so close?

'I cannot imagine a time when you will not be trying to kick over the traces, my dear,' he murmured, and the heat of his breath caressed her skin. She would have stepped away, but he slid his arms around her waist and dropped his mouth to kiss the tender spot above her collarbone. Heat inflamed her. *Is this why Lady Phoebe looked so sad and bewildered by his arrival with me?* Daisy wondered. *Did she relish his touch and know she'd lost him?*

'Reuben,' she gasped, 'what are you doing?'

She felt the rasp of Reuben's chin as he lifted his head. He relaxed his grip, and she wriggled sideways out of his arms until she could turn and lean back against the table. Reuben surveyed her with half-closed eyes. His breathing was more rapid than usual, and she could see he needed a moment to think of a reply.

'Taking a little of the retribution due for that slap,' he said, and she remembered the moment with startling clarity. The moment she'd known without doubt that she could not marry John Brent because she was in love with Reuben Longreach.

'How ungentlemanly of you,' she whispered.

'Maybe, my dear, but how male,' he said. Daisy watched in fascination as a smile grew in his eyes and bloomed.

'How dare you laugh at me?'

Reuben's features settled into serious regard. 'I knew you were too young for marriage, my dear, and I had to separate you from that idiot Brent before you talked yourself into his bed. I could see, if no one else could, that you not only wanted to write novels, but you wanted to live the excitement of them, too.' He brought a hand up and drew it around his neck. 'It was my intention you would never know of Phoebe's role in my life, but your persistence over the visit to the docks meant I had to sacrifice your good opinion. Will you forgive me?'

'You did set out to destroy my betrothal. How can I forgive you for that, even if there was nothing else?' Daisy said. Her voice was low with anger, and she only realised she had revealed her hand when Reuben's eyes took on a wary expression.

'What else troubles you about my character, Daisy? You are older now, and know more of life and a man's needs. I suppose you will have enjoyed a few clandestine kisses after dancing, but I do not probe.' He took hold of her upper arms, and she could not escape the intensity of his stare.

'I am troubled by the way you feel entitled to insult me on any occasion you find me unattended,' she said, and he immediately released her. 'If I cannot sway Toby's decision to give you house room again, then I will accept the offer I expect to receive from Mr Campbell, and insist on an early marriage.'

'No, Daisy. I *will* abduct you if you do anything so mutton-headed. Believe me, my dear. We are meant for each other, and I intend to relieve you of your dilemma as soon as possible.'

'I have no dilemma other than being aware I trespass on my brother's household,' she said, but it was unconvincing even to her own ears.

'Nonsense, my dear. Your dilemma has always been the fire and passion in your nature that vies with society's expectations of a well-bred girl. Now you think you have discovered something else about my character that prevents you from coming to me.' He moved away and set a hand on the door handle.

'Toby and I are in agreement over most issues. He will be told that Mr Pemmican was in the Campbells' company this morning.'

Daisy stood recovering her breath after the door closed on Reuben's tall figure. How dare he expect her to absolve him of everything? And yet, there had been several kisses as she had tried to forget him and find herself a beau. There had also been one or two undignified scuffles when the young man forgot she was not the light-skirt he undoubtedly met with on other occasions. None of that had brought heat flaring through her veins.

She lifted the damaged rose and clipped it short. She would wear it on her dress this evening. Loving Reuben was not enough. If he was in harness with Pemmican to reap what could be reaped from the trust and the family, then she could never have a future with him.

She puzzled over the realisation that had come to her in the park. Reuben could be the connecting link. He had gone to Edinburgh. He had been at the docks. He had met her uncle Howie and Pemmican when no one else was present to hear their conversations.

And now? She closed her fingers around the rose and squealed as a thorn pierced her skin. Now the unworldly Archie Campbell and his devoted sister had been brought into the hideous lawyer's orbit. And that had happened just after they were introduced to the Mellons and Reuben reappeared.

16

'My dear Daisy, you are becoming over-excited,' Toby said with calm finality. Knowing it meant he would not accede to her wishes, she cast him a glance of such exasperation that her sister-in-law laughed.

'Mariah, you must see how all the bits of this puzzle fit together,' she begged. 'You are not bound by imagined loyalty to the opinion of any male.'

'Daisy!' At a younger age, Toby's anger would have caused her to think of a diverting way of turning his thoughts and making a plan, but it was too late for any of that. Reuben had to be confronted, and if guilty, stopped.

'You shout, brother, but you must see the logic of my arguments. While you have been stuck in London or Hampshire with family responsibilities, he has been free to roam and to plot.' She paced the rug in front of the fireplace in her private sitting room. It had been necessary to waylay Toby and Mariah after they came downstairs from the nursery because there was no other gap in their busy schedules.

'I am troubled by your assertion that I favour Reuben's opinion because it is male,' Toby said sternly. 'I am always careful to listen to you and Mama, and to my wife.' He crossed to a window and looked down into the square. Daisy studied the rigid muscles beneath his coat and decided she must change tack.

'That is true. I apologise, but I still do not understand why you are unable to see what our cousin has been about,' she said, and it didn't sound as conciliatory as perhaps it could have.

'I wonder how you come to these resolutions, Daisy,' Mariah said. 'I once made some hasty decisions myself when I was frustrated by the strictures of being female. Sadly, people suffered for it.'

'People did suffer, and you would perhaps have been wise not to go off in such a reckless manner,' Daisy began, but gurgled to a halt. She knew, and should have remembered, that Toby would hear no criticism of Mariah's actions over the Wellwood affair.

'We have extended this discussion long enough,' he said. 'Daisy, I have had a formal request from Mr Archibald Campbell of Argyll to grant him an audience. I am led to understand this has to do with making an offer for your hand.' His features were closed, and Daisy blenched. When he frowned in just that way, it was Reuben's face she saw. Reuben, who had warned her he would abduct her to prevent any such marriage.

'It may be. I find the gentleman interesting, if single-minded,' she said equivocally. Could she marry Archie Campbell? she teased herself once more. There was a more than reasonable chance that boredom would cause her to throw herself into a ravine on his isolated estate.

'What am I to say to him?'

'Toby, my love, you are putting pressure on Daisy when perhaps we have not known Mr Campbell very long,' Mariah said with more reason than the blood relatives were able to show each other. 'Besides, will you not want to ask Reuben why he thinks the Pemmican man was in the park this morning?'

'You, too,' Daisy murmured.

'I do not mean you were mistaken in identifying Mr Pemmican,' Mariah continued, 'but if you believe there is a connection between him and either Reuben or Mr Campbell, then we would be foolish to pursue a liaison while the matter is unresolved.'

Brother and sister gazed at Lady Mellon, and each sank onto a chair.

'My love,' the earl began, 'I am so often reminded how superior your faculties of reasoning are. How could we not have seen that?'

'You are right, Mariah. Thank you.' Daisy sent her sister-in-law a small smile.

A silence matured in the room. Toby stood up at last and, taking out his pocket watch, tutted in exasperation. 'I am minded to agree to Mr Campbell's request, Daisy.' The earl acknowledged a protest from his wife by raising a hand. 'Obviously, my dear, you must not accept an offer from someone with whom you would not suit. It might be a good opportunity for us to discover the extent to which he is in league with Pemmican, and it is good to keep one's enemies as close as possible.'

Daisy smiled shyly at her brother. He was so good to all the family, and yet she was still unable to accept an offer of marriage and allow him and his countess to lead their own lives. She made a mental vow to try harder when they had unravelled the mystery.

'Reuben said you had made an offer to Mariah to host a soirée in honour of an educational scheme,' she said. 'He wondered if Mariah would agree to the scheme being the funding of a plant-hunting expedition. He thought perhaps Mr Campbell might benefit from it.'

'That is an interesting proposal,' Mariah said. 'I have always been keen to pursue basic literacy, but we need to extend the boundaries of knowledge, so those who can read may learn.' Clearly captivated, she smiled up at Toby, and how Daisy envied them in that moment. She would never know such complete understanding with anyone.

'Yes, my love, and the man can name anything he discovers after you,' Toby said with a laugh.

'Even if it has thorns or eats flies?' Mariah teased her husband.

'I expect Mr Campbell's scientific nature will be a problem in realising he needs to find a more attractive plant for his benefactor's wife.'

'But if it does not, his sister's sensibilities are superior,' Daisy said with finality.

She had strong suspicions that Mr Campbell's ardour would diminish sharply when he was in charge of his own travelling fund. Her own allowance would be so much less attractive then. Reuben's ploy was a clever one, but perhaps one way of contemplating marriage with Mr Campbell was to know he would spend much of any year overseas.

* * *

Reuben sat at the pianoforte and picked out some scales. His heart was not in the full-blown practice piece open before him, and soon enough he gave up. A sound behind him brought his head round.

'You are distracted, Reuben.' The earl spoke from just inside the door, and Reuben glanced across. *No more than you, cousin*, Reuben thought with interest. *What have the females done to bring that stern expression to your brow?* He watched Toby move slowly across the room to the big windows that led into the gardens.

'You surprised me,' Reuben said calmly. 'Stephens was keen to explain how long you had been closeted with an agitated Lady Daisy and the countess. I know Daisy is so enamoured of the idea that I am engaged in stealing the family silver, that she might not be easily dissuaded.' He stood and joined the earl. The men could watch little Connie playing with a nursemaid. Daisy and Mariah sat to one side under a tree, and Nanny carried baby Fred around wrapped in a shawl.

'A domestic sight,' Toby observed dryly. 'I do not believe you are trying to steal the family silver. Nor do I entertain the idea that you wish to be the Earl of Mellon. The cousinship is so convoluted, I cannot work out how many lines would have to die out before you inherited, but it is several.' He leant against the window frame. 'Of course, I was unable to tell Daisy and Mariah how much conferring we have engaged in. It may cause them to be suspicious of your intentions and place in the investigations.'

Reuben sighed. 'I have always thought we should have given the ladies more of the information we had, although I know you were circumspect after the way Mariah went for Wellwood.' He met the earl's glare.

'Daisy has a love of the dramatic,' Toby said. 'One has to remind oneself of that when thinking about giving her ammunition to be yet more dramatic.'

'Indeed. On the other hand, six years ago we had two plots to kidnap females of the family, and today Pemmican has reappeared.' Reuben was sure Daisy would have told Toby this, and waited while the earl nodded. 'He was in the park this morning. When I suggested to Daisy that Mr Campbell might benefit from your proposed recital, that young man turned to look at where Pemmican had stood. He was very self-conscious.'

'As if he had allowed himself to agree to a criminal suggestion, and then honest salvation comes along,' Toby observed. He tugged his neck cloth free and pulled it off. Reuben raised an eyebrow in surprise but said nothing.

'I cannot think to allow Daisy to accept his hand now. Whatever he's been engaged in with Pemmican, matrimony does seem to be incompatible with his calling.'

Ah, Reuben thought, *I'm relieved to learn that, but I might still need to act to keep Daisy out of an entanglement.*

'With the utmost respect, Toby, I wonder that you gave the idea more than a passing nod. Daisy and Mr Archie Campbell might tie a knot, but it would almost certainly be around one another's necks,' Reuben said.

'You know why I entertained it. I feel constrained by the presence in the house of its mistress, its former mistress, and a woman who could easily run it with her eyes shut.' Toby sighed. 'You are supposed to be assisting me in this, man, and yet you offer Campbell an escape route.'

'The idea was out before I had time to consider,' Reuben said mendaciously. It would upset Toby a lot if he knew how the problem had exercised Reuben's wits for much of the night. 'His sister was immediately grateful.' He caught sight of Toby's discarded neck cloth, and an inkling of the earl's irritation began to seep into his understanding. 'Perhaps you feel your mama does not spend enough time in the Dower House?'

'The Dower House was redecorated and refurbished, but the dowager has spent no more than three months in it in total. Apparently Mariah could not be expected to cope while producing the heir.' Toby laughed, but it was a grim sound.

'And when the heir was Connie, your mama needed to remain in case the next confinement *was* the heir.' Reuben smiled to take a little of the sting out of his words. 'And now?'

'And now?' Toby squared his shoulders, and Reuben wondered if he'd come up with an idea. 'And now I am out of ideas, unless Mr Stanhold pursues his suit with more vigour.'

I am so glad. Now is my moment to have ideas. Mr Stanhold is not one of them.

'Did you enjoy your reunion with Mr Brent?' Reuben asked.

'I found John less to my taste than he once was, but his wife even more delightful. She told me confidentially that she is to meet up with Daisy in Gunther's parlour tomorrow morning.'

'I wonder why Elspeth thought you needed to know?'

'Because she needed my support in

persuading John it was an acceptable arrangement,' Toby answered. 'He blusters and so forth as he always did, but he remains shaken by how easily you lifted Daisy from under the eyes of all the men in the household.'

They were silent for a few moments before both spoke at once. 'Go ahead,' Reuben said.

'Reuben, could you bear to accompany Daisy to this rendezvous, please? With Pemmican appearing again in plain sight, I am reluctant to allow her out without a proper escort.'

Reuben held Toby's gaze, though he was afraid his own might give away the extent to which he wanted to be in company with Daisy.

'I think I would be able to cope, Toby. I was delighted to learn Brent had agreed to allow his wife back into our society. I have always held Elspeth Howie in very high regard.' The debacle of six years ago had cost much in terms of friendship and society. Surely it was time for them all to swallow a little pride and restore harmony? 'Has it occurred to you, Toby, that securing Daisy in marriage is the only way we are going to frustrate the ploys to kidnap her and ruin her life?'

'Yes,' Toby agreed bleakly. 'And now one of only two candidates of this Season is contaminated. I wonder why no one has tried to kidnap Lady Beatrice?'

'Well, her allowance belongs to her absent husband, does it not?' Reuben asked.

'Of course, but as he languishes on the other side of the globe, it is paid to my aunt.'

* * *

Daisy glared at Reuben as he extended a hand and assisted her descent from the Mellons' town carriage. She was furious with the entire world. Toby did not take her concerns seriously. Mariah suggested she might have got a wrong impression. Reuben simply smiled and, when he knew no one could hear, reminded her she had not told the earl about his snatched kisses.

'You must summon a smile or two for Mrs Brent, Daisy. She has interrupted her first week in London since her children were born to meet you,' Reuben said with the kind of unanswerable logic she particularly disliked.

'How do you know that?'

'Because, Mademoiselle la Shrew, Toby had a note from her husband telling him so.' Having delivered this muddled French, Reuben slid her arm through his and would have set them off across the pavement, but Daisy was brought to a standstill by anger.

'That is without doubt the most patriarchal action the man has made. It is even worse than returning my letters unopened,' she exclaimed.

'Do not stop moving, my dear. It causes congestion for other passers-by.'

'Do you not agree?'

'Of course I agree. Brent would never have made you any kind of suitable husband.'

'That is not what I asked you to agree to; but since you mention it, I told John that when I met with him and Elspeth,' Daisy said, and regretted it immediately. She risked a sideways glance at Reuben, and was further irritated by the broad grin he did nothing to conceal.

'Here is your cousin,' he said mildly. 'It is not my intention to dampen your conversation, so I will take a separate table once I have exchanged greetings.'

If Daisy was surprised by this show of concern for her feelings, she decided to keep it hidden. She really wanted to have a private conversation with Elspeth, and it would be without any sense to object. Toby had made it very clear to her that either she accepted Reuben's escort, or she did not make the expedition at all.

17

'Daisy, my dear cousin, why are you so unhappy?' Elspeth asked as soon as the waiter had set their glacées on the table and moved off.

She had not expected Elspeth to ask such a direct question and was perhaps not as prepared for it as she could have been. The truthful answer, *I think Reuben Longreach is in connivance with Mr Pemmican,* would not serve. 'I have not been sleeping well, and Smithers was saying this morning how the disturbed nights were affecting my looks,' she said instead.

'Smithers takes a great liberty if she feels able to make such remarks to her mistress,' Elspeth said mildly, and Daisy knew she had to take hold of her wandering thoughts. It was very difficult to think clearly when Reuben was situated so close, and her mind was full of the delightful memory of his kiss in the library. It became increasingly hard to breathe evenly. She conjured a picture of Pemmican lurking below the tree, and everything snapped into place.

'Smithers has looked after me well. I will come about, Elspeth, and I hope your good sense will be at my service.' Daisy sat straighter and fixed her most appealing glance on her cousin.

'I am so glad we are able to meet, and of course I am only too happy to assist you in any way. What is troubling you?'

'I am conscious of trespassing on Toby and Mariah's good natures. There have been several young men during the last six years who might have offered for me had I not made it known that I was not ready to marry,' Daisy said.

'Do you require Toby's consent?'

'Yes, but he has never suggested he would withhold it where my affections were settled. My birthday is next week and I shall be twenty-four. Next year, I would —'

'Would not require Toby's approval

because you will be twenty-five,' Elspeth interrupted. 'But surely you would always want to please the head of the family?'

'Of course, Elspeth, but that truly isn't the reason I mention my advancing age. What I am conscious of is this: if I do not marry before my next birthday, Toby and Mariah would be entitled to ask me to leave their house.' Daisy wiped away the tiny tear that had gathered in the corner of her eye. It was truly frightening to contemplate a future of living alone in a small house with only Smithers for companionship.

'Because you will assume control of your fortune?'

'Yes.'

'Daisy, do you seriously envisage your mama permitting such a state of affairs?' Elspeth asked. She stirred the fruit and ice-cream in the bowl in front of her so vigorously that it began to resemble coloured sludge. 'I cannot think it of Toby either.'

'Toby is the very best brother I could want, but he is overset by the number of female personalities in his house — Mama, Mariah, myself, Aunt Mathilde. Mariah's aunt, Mrs Wilson, stayed for three months while Mr Fox was ill.' Daisy picked up her lacy summer gloves and swished them back and forth across the tabletop. 'I wonder if this is why he has invited Reuben to stay after so long.'

'Reuben?' Elspeth lifted a spoonful of the coloured sludge and without looking at it swallowed it. Daisy watched as the other girl's eyes closed in realisation, but Elspeth's manners were impeccable. She said nothing.

'Yes, Reuben. He is everywhere I turn, and after six years of absence, it feels almost as if he's in my hair.'

'What a strange remark, cousin.' Elspeth set her spoon down and sat up straighter on her chair. 'John will, sadly, fret himself into an anxiety if I overrun the time we agreed. Will you try to tell me what I can help you with?'

'Yes. The problem I need your advice over is simple. I have two eligible suitors.

Mr Norman Stanhold, who is the heir of Lord Stanhold, is a bruising rider to hounds. He makes me laugh. Mr Archie Campbell is a plant-hunter and explorer. He spends a great deal of time working abroad. He tells wonderful stories of strange places.'

'Well, cousin, you manage to make them sound a little dull, if truth be told,' Elspeth said thoughtfully. 'I think I would need to meet the gentlemen before I could form a useful impression of their qualities.'

Daisy turned this idea over before replying, 'Both you and John would be most welcome in Grosvenor Square, but from what you say, he would not want to share dinner with Reuben.'

'No, I fear not. Is your sister-in-law holding any evening parties? John might not object to my dropping in were there a card party or such,' Elspeth suggested.

'It is too close to Mr Fox's death for any formal entertaining on that scale. It would have to be a family dinner.' Daisy's spirits wavered. 'Does John visit his mines?'

'The very thing. How clever of you. I've got so used to him going off on such trips that I forget. He will be in Newcastle next week for two or three nights, and he proposes that I should continue in London while he is away.' Elspeth smiled. 'Were Lady Mariah to invite me on Tuesday evening or Wednesday, I would be very happy to inspect your beaux.'

Daisy gripped her cousin's small hands and squeezed them fondly. 'Thank you, Elspeth.'

* * *

Reuben sat across the carriage from a Daisy he was unused to seeing. She was subdued and thoughtful. 'Your meeting with Elspeth has depressed your spirits,' he ventured. Smithers stared out at the crowds, but of course he was conscious of the maid's presence. There always was someone else, except in those rare stolen moments when she was cutting roses or some other such occupation.

'No, I am delighted to find my cousin in good health and so happy in her marriage.' Daisy did not meet his gaze, and he wondered what nonsense was brewing in her overactive imagination. Was she sufficiently persuaded of his guilt that she'd paraded the arguments before Elspeth? He thought not, because although Elspeth had sent him a quizzical glance or two as he handed her into Brent's town carriage, she had not recoiled, as she surely would have done.

'It remains an enduring mystery that any woman should find life with Mr Brent full of delight. However, I must not snipe, as I remember you contemplated it yourself.'

'It is unkind to remind me of a youthful indiscretion.'

'Your ladyship is in the right,' Reuben agreed. 'Besides, it is difficult to see how your cousin could pass up his offer. In the dreadful circumstances of her papa's transportation and her mama's fall from grace, her only options would be Mr Brent's roof or her grandmamma's. Is the senior Mrs Howie alive and disturbing the peace of Edinburgh?'

'Elspeth's grandmamma died five years ago. She took to her bed when my uncle's sentence was pronounced, and did not leave it.' Daisy spoke calmly, although Reuben knew how much harm the old woman had caused her and many of her relatives. 'I think she was living with Aunt Beatrice in the months leading up to the trial. They took lodgings as Toby put them out of Grosvenor Square.'

He leant forward and squeezed her hands. 'I knew that part, my dear. Toby told me how greatly afflicted your mama was, and how he could not allow the demands of family to override his fear for her health.'

'She was greatly afflicted. Why did you keep me hidden for three days?'

'You were barely conscious for the first two, and the wedding had to go ahead. Howie could only be made to desist, despite being in custody, by the knowledge a ring was on Miss Fox's finger,' he said peaceably.

'But my mama must have been in dire straits. That, too, was unkind, sir.'

Reuben contemplated his companion silently for a moment or two. He had sent word to Toby immediately that his sister was alive and in no danger. The earl had decided after a little consultation that it was best to keep her out of sight, and safe, until the ceremonies were completed. Had he hidden that from her, or was she engaging in her usual over-dramatisation?

'Do you think I did not consult with Toby over the best way to proceed?'

'He has always said he did not know where I was being kept.'

Reuben let this comment pass without any observation. Daisy was not saying Toby had lied to her, only that he had not known where she was. 'I saw no reason to drag the lady's name into the public domain, and neither did you,' Reuben countered. 'However, he did know you were safe, and so did the dowager.'

'Her distress was in the forced separation. She said how painful she found it not to be the one to comfort me.' Daisy relaxed her fingers and smiled broadly. 'It also deprived her of the opportunity to ring a peal over me for the escapade of leaving the house in the night.'

'I expect it did,' he agreed.

* * *

'Mama,' Daisy said as she entered the drawing-room in the early evening, 'Stephens tells me Mr Archibald Campbell and his sister will be joining us.'

'Mariah sent a note,' Lady Constanzia replied. 'I am at a loss, Daisy. You cannot wish to marry a man whose only property is a thousand acres of Scottish bog.'

'Now, Mama, we have agreed to be civil to Mr Campbell, if you please.' Toby detached himself from a position at the end of the fireplace, and Daisy caught sight of Mariah nestling in a huge armchair behind him. Her gown was cut from heavy silk in the pale green she was wont to favour. Daisy spied a chain of alternating jade and emerald squares around her sister-in-law's slender neck. Toby was a generous husband.

'His property in Argyll runs with that of his ducal relative, and has a tower house, several farm houses and cottages in plenty,' the earl said repressively, but Daisy held out little hope that her mama would be silenced or even placated.

'Miss Campbell has also mentioned how beneficial the climate is to the growing on of the specimens Mr Campbell brings back with him,' Daisy said helpfully, 'from his plant-hunting expeditions.'

'Plant-hunting expeditions?' Lady Constanzia sent an enquiring glance towards her son. 'Would your sister be expected to travel with such a husband to find plants? I am sure I think this country has quite enough by way of greenery and such.'

'Mama,' Toby said, and already Daisy heard the signs of exasperation there. She saw Mariah's arm lift, and her hand slide soothingly down his thigh.

'Mama, I have not had the honour of an offer from Mr Campbell.'

'I know that, Daisy. I asked a conditional question, I think.'

Daisy sighed. It would surely not be long before her mama lost patience entirely and decided to throw things. She wondered whether Mr Campbell would find that entertaining or off-putting.

'Stephens,' Toby said, 'where is Reuben?'

'Mr Reuben is changing his coat, my lord. He was practising until ten minutes ago.'

'I beg your pardon, Lady Mellon,' Reuben said as a footman ushered him into the room. He crossed to Mariah's chair and bowed. 'I get a little behind with the practising, and then when I do start again, I lose track of time.'

'Reuben, it's a pleasure to have the instruments played so well,' Mariah said gracefully, and Daisy watched his tall figure turn to her mama's tiny frame. Was she mistaken, or did he take a steadying breath before he addressed her?

'Lady Constanzia,' he murmured, and bowed deeply.

'Reuben Longreach. I thought we might be seeing more of you quite soon,' Lady Constanzia said.

'Did you, my lady?' Reuben answered. 'Why so?'

'There is a Mr Campbell,' she replied with startling imperturbability, 'and also a Mr Stanhold.'

'I have not had the pleasure of meeting Mr Stanhold, but I have met Mr Campbell. He is a distinguished plant collector whose sister draws his specimens most beautifully.' Reuben nodded to Anna, her mama's companion, and then turned to her. 'Good evening, Daisy. May I sit with you?'

Daisy drew her skirts aside to let Reuben sink onto the sofa beside her. She lifted her glass and sipped the ratafia wine Stephens had set down for her. It was very distracting to have Reuben quite so close, and she took a moment or two to allow her fluttering pulses to settle. What, she wondered, was the meaning of her mama's observation? Until the attempted abduction of Elspeth Howie,

Reuben had practically lived with them during the Season.

'I have seen some of Susan Campbell's drawings, Mama, and they are very skilful. If we are to go ahead with the subscription evening, then perhaps she could be asked to illustrate the programme?' Daisy spoke as much to deflect her mama's thoughts as anything. She caught sight of Reuben's smile as she turned towards the opening door.

I could wipe that superior expression from your face, Reuben Longreach. How can you really prevent my betrothal to Mr Campbell?

'I trust, Daisy, you will not do anything I need to make you regret later,' Reuben whispered as Stephens brought the Campbells forward to present them.

'What can you mean, Reuben?'

'Precipitate behaviour, my dear. Mr Campbell will be more than satisfied with funding for an expedition.' He stood.

'I suggest, sir, you remember I have a brother who looks to my welfare.'

'Take care. I warned you,' Reuben said

before turning to make Miss Campbell a very civil bow.

The evening passed in relative calm, and Lady Constanzia and her companion went off to her suite after dinner. The younger people retreated to the drawing-room again. Mariah served tea, and Daisy found herself seated with Mr Campbell while the others collected theirs.

'Where would you take an expedition to?' she asked. The young man was all but tongue-tied in her near presence, and Daisy hung onto her patience with difficulty. He had been much more relaxed on other occasions. Daisy wondered whether Reuben had said anything during their morning stroll to upset him. 'Mr Campbell?' she prompted.

'My brother has it in mind to go into the mountains of Siam,' Susan said, casting her brother a warning glare. 'Is that not correct, Archie?'

'Siam? Yes. I heard many good things about the area when I was travelling further east. Siam would seem to be a fertile region.' He blushed so fiercely that Daisy wondered if his skin would be hot should she touch it.

'Siam,' she said, drawing out the vowels. 'The name does sound romantic, does it not, Mariah?'

'As to whether it *is* romantic, Lady Daisy,' Mr Campbell interrupted, 'these places are far-flung, don't you know? And their customs uncivilised. I do not think you would find much to swell a romantic heart among the squalor of their huts and dwellings.'

Taken aback by this loquacity, Daisy smiled a little. Mr Campbell took this as permission to continue. Could he not understand he was contradicting her and preventing any reply his hostess might have hoped to make? She could not bear to glance at Susan, who must be in the depths over his ineptitude.

'The leaders — and there are many below the king himself — have many wives ... '

'Archie,' Susan Campbell said warningly. 'I am sure Lady Daisy understands that foreign states might have habits and practices we in Britain regard as uncivilised or even uncouth. Perhaps it is not the moment to dwell on such.'

Archie, whose complexion had returned to a normal hue, blushed once more, and he reverted to a silence some might have regarded as sullen. Daisy hoped one of the men would rescue the conversation, but across the vast carpet Reuben seemed preoccupied with the condition of his shoes. He straightened the fall of his tightly cut evening coat, and she noticed a bulge near his waist. She knew he had pockets sewn inside his coats so he could carry around rolled-up pieces of music. This bulge, however, had lumps.

Toby sipped his tea, while Mariah said, 'My late papa made a study of the various tribes in those far eastern areas, Mr Campbell. I think I know how very differently they organise their societies.'

'Yes, your ladyship, very differently. Did your papa travel abroad himself?' the young man asked with a touch of diffidence, but without blushing. Daisy wondered if it was only she who reduced him to incoherence. It did not bode well for a courtship or marriage.

'No. Mr Fox had travelled as a very young man, but did not go abroad while the wars with France were raging; and after my mama died, he did not like to leave me unattended.' Daisy saw the frown crease Toby's brow as his wife spoke, and assumed he was moved by her memory of such an affectionate father.

Reuben left his post by the fireplace and set his empty cup down on the tea table. When Mariah looked enquiringly towards him, he shook his head. 'No more, ma'am. I hope you will excuse me, as I am behindhand with my practice,' he said calmly. Daisy saw his right hand slide across his flat waist, and as he turned again, this time towards her and Mr Campbell, he pulled an item from his inside pocket.

'I know you will want this, Daisy, before you retire. For all that the house is so well supplied with rugs, it is easy to find one's feet on exposed wood.' He bowed to Mariah and left the room.

Daisy glanced down and saw her slipper, with its beautifully embroidered cranes, in her hand. She had accepted it without demur, and now it felt as if she had been branded by a red-hot iron.

She stuffed the offending object behind a cushion, but the damage was done. Mr Archibald Campbell would not now be offering for her hand.

* * *

Reuben sat on in the library after the earl left him later that evening. Their exchange had been prickly. Despite his pronouncement the previous evening, Toby had harboured hopes of a betrothal. Now he'd finally conceded that Archie Campbell was not the man for Daisy, and Reuben's actions had saved everyone a lot of tedious posturing.

'The countess remains of the view that a plant-hunting expedition is a good one, however, and I will send Mr Campbell an invitation to join me in White's to discuss it further,' Toby had said as he turned to retire. 'I will also press him on his association with the miscreant, Pemmican.'

'As to that, I have one or two enquiries in the wind. Mr Farquerson and the *Leith Rose* docked yesterday. I will be meeting him while you are with Campbell.' Reuben picked a tune out on the keys of the pianoforte. 'He sent a note in which he referred cryptically to Pemmican's possible departure from London for France. It seems he may need to live where the shadow of the debtors' prison does not fall.'

Reuben played on. Daisy would be infuriated and also embarrassed by his earlier action. What would she think he deserved as retribution for trumping her top card?

The music rose into the darkness of the night and soothed his temper. Daisy was not a child any longer. He could make his move.

18

Daisy lay in her dark room. Something about the evening was troubling her; worrying away at her without ever reaching the surface of her mind. Certainly Reuben had behaved very badly. His flourish with the slipper was the death-knell of any hope that Mr Campbell would come up to snuff.

She sighed. Any young man who had declared himself would have to call Reuben out, and although she thought plant-hunting in wild terrain might call for considerable strengths, she did not think it was an aggressive occupation.

Lady Constanzia had made Reuben a most odd greeting. *'There is a Mr Campbell and a Mr Stanhold,'* her mama had said. What did she mean by such a strange remark?

Daisy threw off her bedding and slid over the edge onto the floor. She shook out her nightgown and crossed towards the embers glowing in her fireplace. What was the niggle?

Lifting a spill, she dipped it among the embers and used it to light some candles. It was comfortable to shift back into the big armchair and bring her feet up below her. She hugged her knees, and letting her lids drop over eyes heavy with sleep, listened to the notes of the pianoforte drift up the main staircase. Reuben was practising, and the memory of that summer six years ago when Toby had found his countess and she had lost her betrothed …

He *wasn't* practising!

The realisation brought her awake and alert in an instant. Reuben was late for dinner, but he had not been at the instrument. She always heard him. The absence of his music was the thing she'd most missed when he disappeared from the household. She had not heard him play this evening while changing and moving around the house before going to the drawing-room. He'd lied to Mariah.

Cold seeped into her muscles, but she could not move. Reuben had a stranglehold on the actions and emotions of every member of the family and the household. Why was she the only person who saw how very duplicitous his behaviour was?

Because he wants to marry me, but he does not want the family to realise it until he's ready to make a move.

Understanding flooded Daisy's brain like the light across the room when Smithers threw open her shutters in the morning. Reuben had been so very careful to keep his romantic attentions hidden. Moments of intimacy snatched behind a closed door, or in the darkness of the summer night, were concealed from the family. She knew how his kisses affected her and left her confused and dissatisfied. She wanted his touch, and that must be to her shame. Reuben was playing her like one of the instruments he'd cherished for years. Even his six years of absence were designed to drive a wedge between her and the unfortunate John Brent.

All his posturing is just that. He needs

my inheritance to carry on playing his music and living the life he does. He might never be in line for the earldom, but he wants to enjoy the same standards through me.

Daisy stretched her muscles and relished the sharp pains they fired around her body. It woke her up to the chaos her thoughts had been in. Reuben had played her, young and unsophisticated, like a violoncello. He'd engineered all the occasions of intimacy that left her trembling and let certain members of the family see her undone by her emotions.

Charlatan.

In the remaining hours of darkness, Daisy plotted revenge.

* * *

'Why, Elspeth, how lovely to see you again so soon,' Daisy said when she met her cousin coming out of the drawing-room in the early afternoon.

'I meant to leave cards for your mama, but she sent for me,' Elspeth said, and raised her merry violet eyes to Daisy's dark ones. If Daisy expected to catch her out in any subterfuge regarding Reuben, she was disappointed.

'Mama has been longing to meet you, and I know since she had reports of the boys from Mariah, to meet them as well.' Daisy glanced at the butler, who was waiting to show Elspeth downstairs. 'I'll ring, Stephens.'

'You have the air of someone with a secret, Daisy.' Elspeth had waited until Stephens was out of earshot.

'Can Mr Brent spare you for a further half-hour? I would have a few words, if you may stay a little longer.' Daisy was relieved to see her cousin nod, and taking her arm through her own, led the way to her private sitting room.

'This is most agreeable, Daisy. A view of the gardens,' Elspeth murmured as she gazed out onto the square. 'You will be able to watch the comings and goings very easily.'

'Toby had it set up for me after Connie was born in order that I might be able to retreat if I wished.' Daisy motioned to a sofa and Elspeth sat down gracefully. How beautiful her cousin was, now she was free from penury and worry. Her skin glowed with health, and her eyes no longer held deep shadows of anxiety. 'I am so glad you and John were able to reach an understanding,' she said, and was enchanted by the quick secret smile and flush of colour the remark brought to her cousin's face.

'It answered my need,' Elspeth said, and Daisy thought it sounded a little careful. 'It is also true that I envied you your betrothal to John — and for that, I must apologise.'

'Please, Elspeth, there is no need. I was simply too young to become anyone's wife. I understand that now.' Daisy smoothed the silk of her gown and sent Elspeth a shy smile. 'Reuben Longreach did try to tell me so.'

Elspeth's expression was instantly guarded, and Daisy wondered whether her cousin was in Reuben's confidence. Drat the man. How could she proceed if he had already secured Elspeth's support?

'Ah yes, Reuben. I fear it will be some time before John agrees to meet with him. He found the meeting with Toby very difficult to deal with, and he came out in red blotches soon afterwards.' Elspeth took a lace-trimmed handkerchief from her reticule, scenting the air with rose, and dabbed her wrists. 'He does still regard Reuben as the villain of it all.'

'Unfortunate for you when the alternative is to argue that one's papa was the villain,' Daisy said in a quiet voice.

'As you say, Daisy. However, Reuben did cause mayhem when he took you out of the mews that night. I have wondered from time to time whether he was pandering to your sense of the dramatic.'

'That is a repressive thing to say, Elspeth. I may have trunks full of my writings,' Daisy admitted at last, 'but I do spend countless hours on a series of activities for the public good.'

'That may be the case now; but when you were not quite nineteen, your head was a little turned by the idea of *fighting* for John's attention, and his hand, was it not?' Elspeth asked, and Daisy saw for the first time how the extremes of her mama's temper were modified in her daughter and became calm good sense.

'You are correct, and it makes me think I have chosen the right person to help me with a plan I have in mind.'

'Lady Constanzia told me of Mr Campbell's defection from his pursuit of your hand. As one who has travelled in the wilder reaches of Argyll, I must make it plain that I would not have visited your establishment there.' Elspeth laughed, and Daisy let a smile spread across her features. How she had missed this woman's companionship. 'However, I now see the problem facing you most clearly. How can Mr Stanhold be brought to make a declaration without Reuben scaring him off?'

'That is indeed the problem,' Daisy said, although the real problem was much larger than forcing a declaration from Mr Stanhold. 'And it is in this matter that I have formed a plan.'

'I am yours to command,' Elspeth said, and the sparkle in her eyes could not have flashed with more intensity. 'Are we to abduct Mr Stanhold and conceal him down in Hampshire?'

'Why no, although that would turn the tables on all these stuffy males in a very satisfying manner,' Daisy said with a nervous laugh. Where had her sensible cousin gone? 'There would be the matter of a special licence. I think the bishop only issues them to men.'

'How frustrating. Tell me, then — what do you want of me?'

'The house you have hired for the Season used to belong to the Duke of Wilmslow, and that gentleman had a reputation among the staff.' Daisy took a deep breath. Her cousin was now a married woman, but she might nonetheless feel Daisy should not know some of what she was about to reveal. 'He installed a false wall at one end of the ballroom.'

'A false wall?' Elspeth exclaimed, and was on her feet in seconds. 'Daisy, get your things. John is with his man of business for at least another hour, and we must view this architectural wonder while you explain the plan to me.'

* * *

Once in the house in Manchester Square, Elspeth dismissed her butler and led the way along a deep corridor to the back of the house. Daisy followed on in some nervous agitation. What if Smithers had been wrong, and she simply looked foolish to her cousin? she wondered.

'Here is the ballroom.' Elspeth opened the double doors into a vast room with pillars and a long series of glazed doors that let onto the back garden down one wall. Children's toys were scattered around with other bits of detritus. 'We have used the space to store belongings not needed all the time, although John has been thinking of holding a dance.'

Daisy scanned the room and could not immediately see what she hoped to see. It was a regular space, and a little dim, as there were blinds covering the doors.

Sunlight fell in slashes across the polished boards of the sprung floor.

'It's square,' she said. 'The room is square.'

'Of course.' Elspeth's voice squeaked. 'It should be a rectangular shape, given the layout of the rooms above.'

With one purpose, the girls scampered across the room till they reached the far end. Daisy halted and gazed up at the solid mass. It was no more and no less than the other two inside walls.

'It's very convincing,' Elspeth said. She ran a hand down the painted wallpaper. 'Silk.'

'Why is there a curtain?' Daisy wondered aloud, and moved to the right where a mass of material fell in folds to the floor. She grabbed a handful of it, and dust rose into the air in a cloud, settling around their heads and shoulders.

Elspeth coughed. 'It must be years since anyone disturbed it.' She waved her hands in front of her face, but the cloud was hardly affected.

Daisy tried again, and the massive

curtain moved a foot or two along the wall, revealing a deep and regular crack down the silk. A sizeable black hole at waist height was let into the wood.

'By gawd, that's for an old-fashioned handle,' John Brent said from behind his wife's shoulder. 'The sort you carried around in your pocket and inserted when you needed to open a secret door.'

Daisy froze. At her side she felt Elspeth still, too, and realised they'd been caught out. She glanced at John's feet where he moved on the spot, and saw he was wearing soft shoes with a very small heel. Unlike the click of their own boots across the parquet, they'd moved his large bulk in silence.

Elspeth recovered her wits more quickly than Daisy could, and turned to reach up on her toes and set a wifely kiss on John's cheek. 'Your man of business has been most efficient today, my dear,' she said. 'My cousin and I were sure we'd have this mystery resolved and hidden away again before you returned.'

'Naughty,' John scolded with such

affection that Daisy felt a sudden shaft of jealousy. She did not hanker after John, though, so it must be jealousy of their relations as she sometimes felt with Toby and Mariah. 'I hope you would not have kept me out of such a delicious scandal. The agent did hint that old Wilmslow was a bit of a rum character. Something about female house staff, but I disregarded it as servants' tales about their betters.'

Daisy's heart jolted. Lucas Wellwood had certainly murdered one parlour maid, and John had professed outrage at the time. Did that lessen if the perpetrator was a duke?

'I mean,' John blustered as if he realised how he'd trespassed, 'it's not as if any of the girls ever came to much harm beyond a tumble …'

'My dear, I do hope you will remember our cousin is as yet unwed,' Elspeth said with the faintest hint of sharpness.

'Apologies, Daisy, apologies. I was simply trying to reassure you that Wilmslow was not throwing anyone downstairs.' John eased his neck cloth with some difficulty. He dropped his hand and let it rest on Elspeth's shoulder. 'Let me make it up to you ladies. Would you like to see inside the room?'

Daisy and Elspeth watched John hurry off to his study and knew they had only a few minutes before he returned.

'I wondered about creating a compromising interlude in this secret room between myself and Mr Stanhold, which you would of course observe, interrupt, and make known to my brother,' Daisy said as quickly as she could form the words.

'I see,' Elspeth said slowly. 'Are you sure?'

'My life is intolerable at present. It can only be resolved by marriage, and Mr Stanhold has certainly made it plain he wishes to marry —'

'Here it is. The agent handed it separately to me with the remainder of the house keys. I had quite overlooked it in the flurry of other activities.' John bustled across the floor. He brought the butler and a footman with him, and candles were lit in readiness in case the room had no window. Daisy and Elspeth stood to one side as their adventure was taken over.

John set the handle into its hole and wiggled it up and down until they all heard a faint click. 'It has settled on its levers,' John said calmly. 'Now . . .' With a flourish, he opened the door, and many years of dust made a veritable curtain out of the chains of cobwebs in the space. The footman swept them aside, and John took a candle before stepping in.

'Well?' Elspeth asked, and Daisy could hear the frustration in her cousin's voice. She felt it, too. John was enjoying his moment of discovery and making it as dramatic as possible. It should have been theirs.

'Not much, really, dear heart,' he said over his shoulder. 'A couple of couches and a table. Looks a bit rickety to me.'

The ladies were able to see for themselves when the butler had shouldered the door fully open.

'Yes,' Daisy murmured. 'Perfect.'

19

The after-dinner group assembled in Toby and Mariah's drawing-room was small for an evening during the Season, but it included the earl and his wife, Daisy, Reuben, Mr and Mrs Linklater, Lord and Lady Stanhold, Miss Eliza Stanhold, and Mr Norman Stanhold. Conversation was lively, and Daisy was able to secure Mr Stanhold's undivided attention.

'I am very grateful to you for the flowers you sent this morning. How could you know scabious are my favourite?' Daisy asked. 'The violet in their petals is delicate, and I like the mass of green stems.'

'I did not know they were your favourite, but they suggested you to me when I saw them in my mother's room last week. Beautiful flower-heads, and dare I say, a slightly untidy mass of foliage, unconstrained.' Mr Stanhold's light grey eyes sparked with humour. 'You are, my lady, an enticing mixture of poise and mischief.'

'Mr Stanhold! If you intend to make me blush, sir, you are succeeding all too well.'

'Then let us talk of less dangerous matters. I enjoyed your brother's description of his visit to Tattersall's. He clearly knows a great deal about how to choose a good horse,' Mr Stanhold said.

'Yes, he does. Have you been out across the Five Fields much? Toby's agent was explaining how advanced the Bills are for building there at last. I think there have been many false starts and hopes over that land.' She smiled. 'London is expanding apace. I cannot think prime areas such as the Five Fields will be left clear for much longer.'

Daisy knew he was interested in building matters. They had met him when an Edinburgh architect delivered a talk about the building of its New Town.

'With respect, Lady Daisy, the building work is underway.' Stanhold smiled. 'I do not think you'll have been out there to see for yourself.'

Daisy felt warmth creep along the back of her neck as it so often did when Reuben was close to hand. He spoke from behind her. 'Are you involved, Stanhold?' he asked civilly. 'I would be most interested to take a tour of the workings if you were able to arrange one.'

Daisy turned to study him and met a challenging gaze. Her hackles lifted. What was he about now? It wasn't as if Mr Stanhold had suggested she might go wandering around building sites.

'I have been once or twice,' Stanhold said with a sideways glance towards his father.

'Your father disapproves?' Reuben asked quietly.

'You can imagine, sir. We have a sizeable estate to run, and he does not wish to see his eldest son turn into any kind of tradesman.' Stanhold sighed, and Daisy wondered what troubled him. Most young men were anxious to be allowed more say about the running of family estates, and fretted when it was withheld. 'He cannot share my enthusiasm for the beauty of a new building.'

'Ah! I think your love of design may match the passion I feel when a score begins to share its secret heart with me and I feel the music ripen beneath my hands.' Reuben smiled and Mr Stanhold smiled back.

'You conjure the feeling exactly, Longreach. Would that my parent understood.' Mr Stanhold looked momentarily cast down, but his good manners prevailed. 'However, it is ungrateful to complain when he seeks to include me in the running of the estate even though he remains vigorous.'

'I may encounter you in White's, and we will hatch a plan,' Reuben said. 'Daisy, as you know, I've been practising for a recital I am to give on behalf of the Foundling Hospital. The committee, through Lady Stanhold, have asked whether you would consent to act as their hostess on the evening.'

Daisy was taken aback by Reuben's request. No doubt the committee, in particular Lady Stanhold, had been guided towards her selection by a suggestion of Reuben's. Clearly, she thought, it was another ploy to keep her close.

'That is a very gracious request, Reuben. Does it refer to Friday evening's event?' she asked while trying to gather her thoughts. Did she wish to be publicly associated with Reuben when she was deeply involved in ousting him from her life? It would appear to be a backward step.

'Lady Daisy,' Lady Stanhold said, coming up to their group, 'I would be honoured to accompany you if you decided to take up the committee's invitation. Like the Longreach family, we Stanholds have been loyal supporters of the work of the hospital.'

Daisy sensed a trap closing, although she doubted Lady Stanhold realised she was being manoeuvred. She cast Reuben a defiant glance. 'Thank you, ma'am. Your company will make the evening pass most pleasantly. We hear much of Reuben's work for many days before a recital, and the playing will hold few surprises.'

Daisy saw the flash of anger in Reuben's deep-set eyes, so like her own. At her side, Norman Stanhold gasped. Had her rudeness shocked him? she wondered. In years to come, when she revealed all of Reuben's duplicity to him, he would understand.

* * *

'Did you hope to draw blood with that unsheathing of your claws, little minx?' Reuben asked, and Daisy halted. They were both walking in the back garden. Daisy had been drawn by a restlessness that would not let her sleep. She could only surmise Reuben was similarly affected although he often came into the garden to smoke before he retired.

The summer night let its perfumes into the air, and there was precious little light to see by. No moon aided them or made them visible to anyone looking out from the house. She could not catch any hint of his expression, but his voice was cold enough to send chills along her nerves.

'Do you bleed?'

'Be careful, Daisy. Rarely have you made me as angry as you did this evening.'

He was clearly offended by her criticism of his skills. It was so difficult to get beneath his urbane demeanour that a tiny flash of success made her speak thoughtlessly. 'Angry? I suppose that means you feel everyone enjoys your playing and rates it in the first rank,' she said. The words were spiteful, and Daisy felt heat suffuse her face. Reuben was an accomplished musician. Attacking him in this way was to little purpose and no credit. She would prevail in their unacknowledged war over her inheritance, and there was no point in making life unpleasant for her family, but some devil drove her.

'Claws again. Sheathe them, or I will take action to render them safe,' Reuben said from only an arm's length.

'You forced this invitation from the Foundling Hospital committee on me,' she said, holding herself still. She would not scamper back to her room. Her right to walk in her brother's garden was stronger than Reuben's.

'If I did, I simply hope to create good relations between you and your future mama-in-law. Is it not the case that you hope to receive an offer from Mr Stanhold?'

'I thank you to keep your hand out of my personal affairs, sir. I have a brother and a mother who look to my best interests,' Daisy spoke with furious intensity. She felt her breathing was constrained by Reuben's closeness.

'And yet you are able to admit Toby's choice in Mr John Brent was an error of judgement ...' He let the words tail away, and Daisy's fury rose to boiling point.

'I will not stay here to be insulted. My words offended your vanity, Reuben —'

'More than that, they cut me to the quick. If I truly believed you did not value my musical skills, Daisy, my life would be worth so much less,' he said quietly.

'Really?'

'Yes, really.' He was much closer now, and she felt his breath tickle some hairs loose on her shoulders. 'Because, my dear, all my music is dedicated to you. There would be no point if you did not value it as I value you.'

Reuben's arms came around her and turned her to face him. She arched back, but his arms were strong and he held her firmly in place.

'Does Stanhold make you squirm in anticipation?'

Daisy's eyes widened in confusion. Reuben had been teasing her, playing her along. She lifted her foot and brought it hard against his shin, wriggling out of his embrace when he recoiled.

'Mr Stanhold's attentions to me are no business of yours, sir. However, it is time my brother was told of the way you seek me out to manhandle me. I will inform him in the morning.' She turned to step back into the library. 'I am sorry you have laboured under any misapprehension, but I do not value your music. It remains unclear to me why a score sounds the same if played by you after hours of so-called practice and when played by a local organist with the most rudimentary skill.'

She felt the breath seep from Reuben and knew her words had hit home. She would not be manipulated any more. Norman Stanhold was her choice, and this time, she would have him.

* * *

Daisy entered Toby's study the following morning and was immediately struck by his sombre expression. Had something happened to their mama during the night? Had Mariah been taken ill?

'Good morning, Daisy,' Toby said. 'Sit down, please.'

'Is my sister quite well?' she asked.

'Mariah is a little sick to the stomach, but no more than when she expected Connie. If I am a little downcast, it is because I have news concerning Aunt Beatrice.'

'Aunt Beatrice?'

'Yes. It's a little complicated, as ever. A letter from the Pemmican man came during the night. Our uncle died soon after Christmas of 1826.' Toby lifted a sheet of paper and replaced it on his desk. 'News takes an unconscionable time to drift back from the colonies.'

'So Aunt Beatrice is now a widow?' Daisy said.

'She is, and Pemmican has already taken steps to inform her. He continues to act for Mr Howie as of right.' Toby brought his clenched fist down on the desk and Daisy jumped. 'As if the man has not caused this family enough distress, he carries on regardless.'

Daisy swallowed. This did not seem to be a good moment to present her complaints about Reuben. Toby was worried about the effects of her aunt's widowhood, and with good cause, she thought. Aunt Beatrice was now in sole control of a large annual income. Her obdurate character, coupled with resentment at being removed from the family circle, might tempt her into any number of schemes or indiscretions.

'I'm sorry, Daisy; you wanted to consult me about something?' Toby made a visible effort to relax, and Daisy's heart went out to him. She could not add to his burdens at present. Reuben was bested for now, but she determined that if he made any further overtures, she would scream and bring the household down around his ears.

'I did, but it is of little import in comparison with the news about Mr Howie.' She smiled and stood up, straightening the front of her gown. 'I will not trouble you. Perhaps I'll visit Mariah and see whether she would benefit from a turn in the fresh air.'

'That would be a kindness, as I don't envisage being able to offer you ladies escort today. Josh will accompany you,' Toby said. 'Reuben has been kind in making his time available, but he departed this morning, very early.'

'Has he gone back to his lodgings?' Daisy asked. This was what she wanted, and she was out of patience with the sharp pang of disappointment she felt on hearing the news.

'No, to Portman Square,' Toby said as

if she should know what that meant. In response to her puzzled expression, he continued, 'How stupid of me. You have not been party to the events in Reuben's life over the interval since my marriage. Reuben inherited the estate of his mama's much older brother. It is substantial.'

'Reuben is wealthy?' Daisy asked. She felt the certainties of her life crumbling. Could she have been mistaken? Could it be that Reuben was one man who wanted to marry her and had no need or regard for her fortune?

'Very wealthy. It was an inheritance which was not always going to come to him, but his uncle lost his first wife and two small boys to illness. The second Mrs Critchely died twenty months ago, and Reuben came fully into the properties.' Toby smiled. 'There must have been reports in the *Times* and the other tattle sheets. How did you miss them, my dear?'

'How indeed?' Daisy asked. Though missing them was no surprise, as she'd avoided any headline with Reuben's name in it. 'Of course, I don't recognise

Critchely. Mrs Longreach's name was Bentworth, was it not, before she married?'

'Yes, I think it was. Mr Critchely was her half-brother.'

Daisy hardly knew where she found the strength to leave Toby's study and return to her room. Any thought of exercise was abandoned while she came to grips with this news.

If Reuben had no need of her inheritance, then perhaps his words in the garden were not teasing, but the result of genuine hurt. Perhaps Reuben did want to marry her because he loved her.

Daisy threw herself onto the bed and buried her face in the spread. So much that had been foggy and dark was clear now, to the point where she wanted to scream. She grabbed a cushion from a bank of them piled up on her bolsters by the maids and mangled it between her hands. Why had she been so obtuse, so stupid, so ... She thought of the ridiculous idea of compromising Mr Stanhold ... So childish?

Pride.

'My lady?' Smithers asked in a voice shaking with fright. 'My lady, you've destroyed that cushion. Let me take it, please.'

Gently Smithers removed the mess of feathers and silk from Daisy's arms and drew her up into a sitting position. The maid waited, but Daisy was unable to move or speak, so great was the shock.

She loved Reuben — but she had done everything possible to drive him away. She had allowed his dalliance with Lady Phoebe to become a barrier between themselves, and that was her dilemma. How could she resolve it?

20

Reuben shifted from one booted foot to the other. It might be midsummer, but around the docks the wind was chill and a man needed to keep moving.

His heart was frozen, but he needed to resolve this muddle for Toby. Once he'd discharged his duty to the family, he could truly separate himself. How he'd miss Toby — but he must give him up, too, if he hoped to avoid Daisy.

'Longreach,' Farquerson called in a guarded fashion from beneath the overhang of an alehouse. 'Let us go inside, man.'

The two young men entered a dark, low building full of smoke from a dozen or so pipes and a struggling fire. Farquerson ordered ale for them both and led the way to a secluded corner where tall stools were set around a wobbly table. They drank deeply so their glasses would not spill when they set them down, and studied each other in the gloom.

'It's not as salubrious as you'll be used to, Mr Longreach.' Farquerson nodded at their surroundings.

'I can cope, sir. You have news of the earl's aunt.' Reuben knew he was short, but in truth, he could not raise his spirits this morning. Daisy's cruelty stung, and the memory of her words baited him.

Farquerson waited a moment or two before speaking again. 'A woman, is it? They can be the very devil, and particularly tiresome in introducing an obstacle just as you thought you'd cleared a path and strewn it with bluebells.'

Reuben stared at the man. How had he got so quickly at the heart of things when Reuben had never given him any indication of his personal dealings? 'You mistake the matter, Farquerson. The young lady condemned my playing skills. I am left to reflect that perhaps I value myself too highly, and have been imposing noise rather than music on my audiences for years.'

'Well if that's all, then I can't see the problem. My brother plays the bagpipes, and his wife makes him take them up the glen to practise. I came myself to hear you play one time when the *Leith Rose* was in town. If the young lady doesn't like the music you make, she must be tone-deaf.'

Reuben took a slow mouthful of ale. Farquerson never failed to amaze him with his insights and ambitions. He'd yet to hear why the man was saving his bribes and commissions so zealously, but it might be something surprising.

'The earl asked me to give you this,' Reuben said at last, closing the subject of women. He handed Farquerson a bag of guineas. 'What news do you bring him?'

'Aye. Not so good this time. Mr Pemmican was around in Berwick. I caught a glimpse of him from the harbour, and there was a lady on his arm. My suspicion is that the lady was your man's aunt, Lady Beatrice, because it was around the time news of Mr Howie's death came back.'

'When did this become known? The earl only received news of it from Pemmican last night.' Shock made Reuben give away his hand, although he'd become so used to Farquerson over the years that he didn't see things that way any longer.

'At least three months ago, Mr Longreach. We missed each other when you were touring in the Low Countries.' Farquerson sounded thoughtful. 'That lawyer is up to no good in respect of the lady, I'll bet.'

'Lady Beatrice?' What had Toby said when they discussed Daisy's marriage plans? *'Why does nobody abduct Lady Beatrice?'*

The Lord save us from our desires, Reuben thought.

He took a moment or two to recover from the confusion caused by learning how stale the news Pemmican had sent to Toby was. Farquerson ordered up another couple of tankards, and Reuben took his without thinking.

'I must make it known to you, Mr

Longreach, that I am resigning my post with the *Leith Rose*, and indeed, with the company.' Farquerson sat straighter on his stool.

'You are?' Reuben muttered. 'Are you going to another?' It probably didn't signify, as Lady Beatrice was apparently not now living in an east coast port. Toby would be in need of information from other, perhaps London-based, sources.

'No, sir. I am setting up a school in Scotland. I have a piece of land with some foreshore, and together with my brother I am going to train lads for the sea.' Farquerson spoke with pride, and Reuben saw how his face was set in determination. This, then, was the key to one riddle.

Reuben drank some more ale and then set his tankard aside. He'd eaten nothing before leaving Toby's house and found no reason to dally in his own. The servants weren't looking for him at six o'clock. His head felt a little woozy.

'Are you quite well, Mr Longreach?' Farquerson asked, and Reuben heard the concern in the other's voice. 'Did you breakfast before setting off?'

'To tell the truth, I am in need of some sustenance, Farquerson.' Reuben made an effort to concentrate. 'I wish you well in your new venture. I have often thought the lads are too young and inexperienced to go straight from dry land to a heaving deck. Your idea is a sound one.'

'Thank you, sir. I hope to welcome you there in the future to see how it goes on. You must realise this is what I've been reserving these *gifts* of his lordship's for over the years.' Farquerson raised a hand and one of the men came from the bar. 'The gentleman would like some bread.' He dug a few coins from his jacket and gave them to the serving man. 'Fresh rolls and beef. Go out for it.'

'That's thoughtful of you, Farquerson, but there's no need,' Reuben said, although his head was thick and the room seemed even darker.

'You always dealt fairly with me, sir. I'll not be letting you wander off into these narrow streets with a muzzy head.'

Farquerson regarded him patiently. 'Now, sir, begging your pardon, but I'm thinking it would be a good idea if you were to tell me how the lady has reduced you to wandering the streets of the docklands with no regard for your personal safety.'

Reuben picked up his tankard, thought better of drinking anything further before eating, and set it down again. Farquerson's weather-beaten face was intelligent and calm. He'd make a good instructor and mentor for the boys leaving home for the first time.

'You do, man, do you?' Reuben said.

'Aye, sir. Sailors may not have a lassie in every port, as the popular sayings go, but we meet a few.'

'She's beautiful, Farquerson, but oh so wilful.'

'And a man like yourself, growing up with wealth and the freedom to indulge it, and used to schooling horses — cannot handle wilfulness?' Farquerson raised his eyebrows and Reuben blushed a little. 'That tells me you have something nagging your conscience, and it's of major proportions.'

'The lady discovered I had a liaison of some years' standing, and she has set it between us.' Reuben was surprised by the words, but once spoken, he knew they were true.

'What is popularly called keeping a mistress?'

'Except that lady was, and remains, a widow, and well provided for. I did not *keep* her, although it goes without saying, I made her a gift or two.' Reuben stalled. Why was he telling this man his innermost secrets? The smell of roast beef wafted from his side, and he took the paper-wrapped food from the serving man.

'The family jewels?'

Reuben's mouth was now full of his breakfast, and so he shook his head. He had not given Lady Phoebe any of the family jewellery.

'Then, sir, here is my suggestion.'

* * *

'Daisy, Daisy,' Mariah spoke anxiously from her bedside, and Daisy choked back a sob. 'I was on the landing when I heard your distress. What is the matter?'

'Mariah.' She clutched her sister-in-law's hand. 'I have been so very stupid and wilful, I think.'

Daisy watched as Mariah's expressive face showed a flurry of competing emotions. It was hardly fair to submit her to such an unreasonable tirade. How could the countess reply and give a tactful answer?

'My dear, I am at a loss. Shall I send for Lady Constanzia?'

'No!' Daisy's voice was a near scream, and she slid from the bed. 'No. I beg your pardon, Mariah, but I think perhaps you and our cousin, Elspeth, are the best people to advise and help me. Mama would be out of all patience, and perhaps justly so.'

'I cannot think that we will get any help from Elspeth today, as Toby has received word of her papa's death.' Mariah stretched out a hand, and taking the hair-brush Smithers was holding, motioned to Daisy to sit before her mirror. 'He has just gone over to Manchester Square to tell her.'

'Yes, I had forgotten. Toby did tell me. That shows how selfish I can be.'

'Daisy, please — I am seriously worried by your distraction. What is the issue?'

Smithers busied herself with tidying the bed, and Daisy wondered whether to ask her maid to go — but didn't she already know more about Daisy's life than anyone?

'I have acknowledged a truth I learned many years ago, Mariah. I am in love with Reuben Longreach.' Mariah's hand stayed, and Daisy felt a tug as the brush caught among the abundant locks of hair tumbling down her back. 'I knew it that summer when you and Toby were married, but as I was busy being betrothed to John Brent and trying to fix Reuben's attentions to our cousin Elspeth, I did not acknowledge it.'

Above her head, Mariah's cool gaze

studied her in the mirror. A shadow — of pain? Daisy wondered — crossed her sister's beautiful face. 'I see,' she said, and Daisy heard the tiny flicker of accusation. Was this how it would be? Would the whole family condemn her for her waywardness?

'Of course, I cannot now accept an offer from Mr Stanhold,' Daisy said, 'but I will prepare to find a suitable companion and a small house to move into. It will be lonely at first, I think, but I will get used to it, and you and Toby will be able to live the lives you truly want to live.' She lifted her chin and squealed as the brush became ever more entangled. Smithers stepped forward and brought a chair for Mariah to sink onto. She took the brush out of the countess's hands and began to restore order to Daisy's locks.

'Daisy, I do not condemn you, my dear,' Mariah said. She set her hand on her waist and Daisy knew a pang of remorse. How could she expect her sister to deal with her idiotic behaviour when she was carrying another infant and was unwell from time to time?

'Thank you. I think that is more kindness than I deserve.'

'Nonsense.' Mariah was vehement. 'I have always felt that Toby, Reuben, and Lady Constanzia try to keep too much from you. If Toby has a formidable intelligence, why might his sister not shine too? You come of exactly the same stock.'

'We do, but think on this, Mariah: I have not been educated as you or the men have. I can read and write, certainly, and I make up my accounts with accuracy, but I have not been able to develop ways of thinking such as you did under your papa's tutelage.' Daisy squirmed as Smithers straightened up and looped her heavy strands of hair into a twist. It was at last secured in place, and Smithers brought a damp cloth to wipe away the traces of Daisy's tears.

'This is undeniable, my dear, but not your fault. It pains me to reflect how even a man like Toby, or Reuben, regards the female as second-class.'

Daisy was relieved to know she was

not the cause of Mariah's earlier distress. 'What is my fault, Mariah, are the stories I have spun out of the material I did have. And what is very much my fault is the hurt I caused Reuben yesterday evening. He may not forgive me.' Daisy felt a trickle of ice settle on her spine. *He may not forgive me* sounded like a death sentence.

'You hurt Reuben? I conclude you criticised his music in some way,' Mariah said, and in the mirror Daisy saw her exasperation. She nodded.

'I said I did not understand how pieces sound the same when played by him after weeks of practice as they do when played by any local organist with rudimentary skill.' Daisy's voice caught on a sob.

'Oh, my. He may not forgive you.'

* * *

Reuben was shown into Toby's study by Stephens and poured a large measure of brandy. 'His lordship may be a little time, sir, as he has gone to acquaint Mrs Brent with the news of her papa's demise. He has said you are always welcome to wait in here, but her ladyship is in the morning room with Lady Constanzia and Lady Daisy, should you wish to join them.'

Reuben glanced at the elderly butler's concerned expression over the rim of his brandy glass. He had not gone home to change, and so was still dressed in last night's evening clothes with yesterday's growth on his normally clean-shaven chin.

'I look disreputable, Stephens, and would do Lady Mellon no credit were she to receive any callers,' he said at last.

'That is not for me to say, sir. I know you went off in search of Mr Farquerson on behalf of his lordship, and so I am sure your mission was urgent.' The butler bowed and began to turn towards the door.

'Stephens, if I may be so bold, would you ask Perkins whether he would shave me and assist me into some of my clean clothes? I take it my things have not yet gone back to Portman Square?' He had decided to make good use of the time

Toby was out and render himself presentable. It was all very well to go off on secret trips among the alleys and docklands, but there was no excuse for bringing the dishevelment back to his cousin's house.

'Mr Perkins will be only too pleased to do so, sir. Why don't you go upstairs to your room, and I will send him to you.'

Within half an hour, Reuben felt more restored. His breakfast of beef and bread had cleared his head, and hot water and clean linen tidied his appearance. He thanked Perkins and walked briskly along the corridor from the bachelors' quarters towards the main landing at the front of the house.

Toby's voice carried up the stairwell in reply to Mariah's softer one, and Reuben sighed. Any hope he'd had of setting up such a domestic establishment with Daisy was shattered by her honesty. How could he set aside his passion for music, even if she truly hated it?

Farquerson's idea tumbled around in his head. 'The lady may not hate your music, Mr Longreach, or even believe you play badly. She may have taken up a position with regard to your romantic liaison that she is unable to understand or shake off,' he'd said, with such composure that Reuben was momentarily convinced. On the other hand, Daisy had had nearly six years to entrench her views, and she was currently pursuing Mr Stanhold.

'Shake up yer ideas, then, man,' Farquerson had said with a belly laugh that threatened to blow Reuben backwards. 'Rivals in love must look to their backs, is what I think. What would the lady find irresistible, in your view?'

'She might like to be abducted by the right gentleman with a special licence in his pocket,' Reuben had mused aloud. He'd told Daisy he would abduct her if she was feather-brained enough to contemplate a union with Archie Campbell. Stanhold was an altogether more serious challenge, and Daisy was very fond of him.

'Do you have a special licence in your pocket, sir?'

'No, but I would take the lady to my

sister until I was able to procure one.' Reuben remembered the light in Daisy's eyes when he'd told her he would abduct her. Was it defiance, or excitement?

'Having a sister is a most useful circumstance for a gentleman in need.'

Reuben's thoughts were interrupted by loud thundering on the front door. Josh and two of the tallest footmen moved forward as one, and Reuben craned over the banister rail. Lady Beatrice advanced into the hall like a ship under full canvas, and to her rear floated Pemmican.

He looks so much more the thing, Reuben thought as he saw the lawyer's well-cut new coat, tailored pantaloons and burnished tall hat. He was dressed as a gentleman, though Farquerson had been adamant his debts were pressing and his creditors more so.

'I think,' Daisy said at Reuben's elbow, 'that charlatan has married my aunt.'

21

'What?'

'I think if Mr Pemmican had been deprived of opportunities to milk any of the family funds through Mr Campbell, my aunt would be a good place to start again,' Daisy whispered, but she knew Reuben heard every word.

'It makes sense in a twisted sort of manner. Why would you risk kidnapping a lady if you could marry her and take over control of her assets?' he whispered back.

The air smelled of sandalwood and tobacco. It teased Daisy's senses as she kept close to Reuben's side. In the hall Lady Beatrice began to look around, and the concealed couple sank as one to their knees, taking their heads below the line of sight.

'Toby did warn Campbell off,' Reuben said, and Daisy thought he might be stalling for time. What should they do now? Descend and listen in on the ensuing fracas Lady Beatrice would undoubtedly cause, or leave the house by one of the back stairs?

'I am tempted to eavesdrop on my aunt's visit, but I continue to detest her so much that even the obligation to assist Toby does not rouse my sense of duty,' Daisy said.

'I am only here to tell him of a possible plan by Pemmican, and that appears to be overtaken by its fulfilment.' Reuben shifted his weight, and when the party downstairs began to move towards the library, they both stood up again.

'Reuben,' Daisy began, and quailed instantly as his deep chocolate-coloured gaze fixed on her face. 'You stare at me as I imagine a starving man might gaze on food.'

That brought a change. Reuben was instantly alert, and she felt his long musician's fingers close around her arm and turn her away from the main part of the house towards the back stairs.

'Where are we going?' she asked.

'I, too, feel my aversion to Lady Beatrice is sufficient reason for leaving the earl to deal with her himself. I cannot think you will return to find she has become welcome in this house, Daisy,' Reuben argued as he urged her downstairs.

'No. She may believe such a marriage would give her respectability, but her collusion with my uncle and his mama will not be forgiven by Toby or my mama.' They had reached the bottom of the stairs, and instead of turning into the kitchen corridor, Reuben opened the area door. The dust-laden air of Grosvenor Square blew around them as they climbed up to the flagged walkway. Late-morning traffic rumbled past, and Daisy noticed a hackney cab drawn up behind a wine merchant's dray. No doubt they had arrived in that, Aunt Beatrice and her ... Must she call Pemmican Aunt Beatrice's husband?

'I will never call him 'Uncle',' she said with emphasis.

'Of course not. And I will never permit you to be in his company,' Reuben said.

Before Daisy could reflect on such an odd remark, he lifted her from her feet and tossed her onto the back of the dray. A heavy canvas covered her over, and within seconds the horses were urged on.

Daisy struggled beneath the weight of the canvas, but it was impossible to free herself. Reuben had at last succeeded where others had tried and failed.

He'd abducted her.

* * *

Travelling through London on the flatbed of a delivery vehicle was unpleasant and slow. Daisy knew some rugs had been strewn across the planks of the dray, but they did little to ease her discomfort. The canvas covering was weighted along the sides and at her feet, but Reuben had lifted the top a little to allow air into her prison.

'I see you can breathe, my dear.'

'Little you care,' she retorted as he dropped the canvas with a laugh to leave her once more in darkness. They spent a long time rumbling among the morning deliveries, and then the vehicle stopped and she heard feet hit the flags of a street. After a short interval, she was lifted from the dray and carried inside the canvas roll. Two men made swaying progress as their arms encircled her at the shoulders and ankles. She was laid on a floor, feet shuffled off, and she heard a door open and close.

'Your delivery, sir,' a voice said, and Daisy thought a Scotsman spoke.

'I wish you well with your new career. Mrs Longreach and I will come as soon as you are ready to receive visitors.'

More footsteps and that door again, opening, closing. Daisy listened and made mental notes. Who could have guessed she would find herself in this predicament? Just as she'd begun to realise what her true *feelings* for Reuben were, he showed his true *colours.* How was she to resolve this?

* * *

Strong hands gripped one edge of the canvas and pulled. Daisy rolled free and struggled into a sitting position. Her skirts were filthy and dishevelled, and her recently styled hair was loose down her back. She removed several pins that were sticking into her neck before lifting a questioning gaze to her abductor.

Reuben extended a hand, which she ignored. She dragged herself up with as much elegance as she could manage and faced up to him. 'How dare you?'

'Oh, I've been planning it for some weeks now, my lady. Would you like something to drink? Water, perhaps? It must have been —'

'Reuben!'

'Oh, my dear,' Reuben said, and enfolded her in his arms. His mouth covered hers in a kiss of such passion that Daisy saw stars behind her closed lids and clung to him for support lest she tumble back to the floor.

Reuben broke the kiss, and Daisy opened her eyes to see the questioning laughter in his. He bent, and tucking his hand below her knees, lifted her. Crossing the room quickly, he shouldered open a door and brought Daisy into a well-appointed morning room. Light blazed through tall windows, and she watched dust motes dance.

Reuben chose a small sofa and sank onto it with her still cradled. She let her head fall against the front of his coat. His arms relaxed and one hand soothed her back. The other lifted her tumbling hair and set it across her shoulder. He gripped her by the chin and lifted her head to place a tantalisingly brief kiss against her lips. She made a small moue of protest, but he was firm.

'My dear, we must have a sensible discussion.'

'Must we, sir?' Daisy asked, though she was secretly both pleased and relieved that Reuben wished to talk to her at all. 'As I am your prisoner, I have little choice but to obey.'

'I am very glad to hear your promise of obedience even before the vicar asks it of you, Daisy, my love, but I hold out little expectation of it being a regular occurrence.' Reuben set her onto the sofa and stood up. He crossed the room to a sideboard and poured two glasses of brandy. 'I think it will help if you sip a little of this. It cannot have been pleasant travelling for so long wrapped in Farquerson's old sail cloth.'

'Indeed, pleasant it was not, Reuben Longreach. Please tell me what this is all about,' Daisy said, although she was beginning to form an idea of his motives. Had he not often referred to her writings and dramatic nature?

'I saw Mr Farquerson of the *Leith Rose* early this morning. I was on Toby's business, and had gone to the docklands without breaking fast. A tankard of ale proved unsettling, and Mr Farquerson wheedled out of me the reason for my unhappiness.' He placed a glass in Daisy's hand and stood in front of the open fireplace. She looked into his face. The seriousness of his expression made her returning confidence falter.

'Was my intemperate outburst

yesterday evening the cause of your unhappiness?' she asked with a tremble in her voice. She sipped a little of the fiery spirit and coughed.

Reuben nodded. He, too, drank a little of his brandy. 'I was desolate to think that all the effort I had expended over so many years was wasted.'

'No!' she cried in real distress. 'I was completely at fault, Reuben. I have misconstrued everything.'

'What is everything?' he asked.

Daisy took another sip of the sustaining liquid and then a deep breath. 'I did try to fix your interest in my cousin, Elspeth. I was not wholly honest in telling Toby about the three days when I missed his marriage ceremony. I did believe you had dealings …' She stopped and raised stricken eyes to Reuben.

He smiled and waited. It gave her the chance to find her courage.

'I did work out that you must have had dealings with Pemmican, and that was why he reappeared when Mr Campbell began to show an interest in me. It seemed all to fall into place, because you lied to Mariah when the Stanholds came to dinner.'

'Daisy! I have never lied to the countess.' Reuben was both puzzled, and she thought, a little offended.

'You said you were delayed by your practising, but you had not been playing. I always hear you. It was so lonely in the house after you moved out six years ago.' She begged him to understand why her thoughts had become so arranged against him.

'Ah, yes. I *was* practising, but not in Grosvenor Square. I had gone to the hall where I will play on Friday evening in order to try their instrument.' A smile lit up his face. 'Goose,' he added.

'Oh,' Daisy said, and hope flooded her. 'I suppose I may have misunderstood some other issues?'

'Daisy ...' Reuben sounded severe. 'I must ask you to tell me everything, because that is the only way we will be able to start recovering from the events of six years ago.'

'Must I say it?' she asked; and then,

because she was not a girl with a head full of silly romances, she answered her own question. 'Of course I must say it. I was jealous of Lady Phoebe Sandison. It made me a little irrational, I think; and when I would have recovered some sense, you had been excised from life in Grosvenor Square.'

Reuben set his glass on the marble shelf above the fireplace and crossed to kneel in front of her. Daisy dropped her own glass and watched in dismay as the remaining brandy soaked into the carpet.

'Lady Daisy, will you do me the greatest honour a humble musician might ask, and agree to become my wife?'

'Yes, Reuben. Yes.'

'My love,' he said as he rose and lifted her with him into a long kiss that sent their quarrels into oblivion. There was a certain amount of disturbance elsewhere in the house, but neither paid it any attention until the door of the morning room was thrown open and people fell in.

'Reuben, unhand my sister, sir!' the earl exclaimed.

Reluctantly, Daisy thought, Reuben released her and turned to face Toby. Mariah, Elspeth and Lady Constanzia crowded through the door, and behind them Daisy could see a footman and a woman, who might be Reuben's housekeeper, hovering.

'Don't be so pompous, Toby, please,' Reuben said, and Lady Constanzia laughed.

'I laugh, Reuben, but my son has a point. Why are you holding Daisy in this manner?'

'Daisy has consented to be my wife.' Reuben took her hand and tucked it into the crook of his arm. 'She always was going to be my wife; it simply took a little organising to arrive at this happy state of affairs.'

'You have not sought my permission,' Toby said.

'Tobias! Now I must agree with Reuben, you are being pompous.'

'Am I, Mama? Daisy has been vociferous in her pronouncements about not marrying Reuben. How do we know she has not been coerced into this? The room reeks of brandy.' Toby delivered this speech while maintaining every muscle of his face in a serious expression, and Daisy began to wonder whether he was in earnest.

'I dropped a glass,' she said. 'Toby, I *do* wish to marry Reuben and listen to his playing ... every night, forever.'

Other titles in the
Linford Romance Library:

SUMMER'S DREAM

Jean M. Long

Talented designer Juliet Croft is devastated when the company she works for closes. She takes a temporary job at the Linden Manor Hotel, but soon hears rumours that the business is in financial difficulties — and suspects that Sheldon's, a rival company, is involved. During her work, she renews her friendship with Scott, a former colleague. At the same time, she must cope with her growing feelings for Martin Glover, the hotel manager. Trouble is, he's already taken . . .

SEEING SHADOWS

Susan Udy

Lexie Brookes is busy running her hairdressing salon and wondering what to do about her cooling relationship with her partner, Danny. When the jewellery shop next door is broken into via her own premises, the owner — the wealthy and infuriatingly arrogant Bruno Cavendish — blames her for his losses. Then Danny disappears, and Lexie is suddenly targeted by a mysterious stalker. To add to the turmoil, Bruno appears to be attracted to her, and she finds herself equally drawn to him . . .

A DATE WITH ROMANCE

Toni Anders

Refusing to live in the shadow of her father, a famous TV chef, Lauren Tate runs her own cake shop with her best friend, Daisy. Having been unlucky in love, Lauren pours her energy into her business — until she meets her handsome new neighbour, Jake, who is keen to strike up a friendship with her. Will Lauren decide to take him up on the offer? Then Daisy has an accident, and announces she'll be following her partner to America once she has healed — leaving Lauren with some difficult choices . . .

ALL BECAUSE OF BAXTER

Sharon Booth

When Ellie's marriage unexpectedly ends, she and her young son Jacob seek refuge with Ellie's cousin Angie. But Angie soon tires of her house guests, including her own boisterous rescue dog, Baxter. When Baxter literally bumps into Dylan, Ellie dares to dream of a happy ending at last. But time is running out for them, and it seems Dylan has a secret that may jeopardise everything. Must Ellie give up on her dreams, or can Baxter save the day?

FESTIVAL FEVER

Margaret Mounsdon

Fleur Denman is given the chance of a lifetime to front the Ridgly Parva Arts and History Festival — but some locals have long memories, and aren't prepared to overlook the scandal that once blackened the Denman name. In the face of adversity, Fleur sets out to prove her worth. Then some festival money goes missing, and Ben Salt, the main sponsor, is among the first to point an accusing finger in her direction. To make matters worse, Fleur finds herself increasingly attracted to him . . .

HEART OF THE MOUNTAIN

Carol MacLean

Emotionally burned out from her job as a nurse, Beth leaves London for the Scottish Highlands and the peace of her aunt's cottage. Here she meets Alex, a man who is determined to live life to the full after the death of his fiancée in a climbing accident. Despite her wish for a quiet life, Beth is pulled into a friendship with Alex's sister, bubbly Sarah-Jayne, and finds herself increasingly drawn to Alex . . .